LEGACY

JAY REACE

First published in the United States of America by FJR Publishing LLC, 2020.

Text copyright © 2020 by Jay Reace

ISBN 978-1-7348990-0-9

Book written by Jay Reace
Book edited by Monique Fischer

Printed in the U.S.A.

Always do as much good as you can, with as little harm to others as possible.

- Victoria Moran

Hey Amanda,

Thank you so much for joining my live & having a little fun. I hope you enjoy my novel & it brings a smile on to your face bigger than the smile I get from seeing your TikTok videos.

Jay
Reace

A SCION BOOK SERIES

LEGACY

JAY REACE

Legacy: A Scion Book Series
Table of Contents

Prologue
Chapter 1: *The Message*
Chapter 2: *Miss Lupita*
Chapter 3: *The Prodigal One*
Chapter 4: *The Journey*
Chapter 5: *A King's Request Part 1*
Chapter 6: *A King's Request Part 2*
Chapter 7: *The Scion's Quest*
Chapter 8: *A Grand Entrance*
Chapter 9: *At All Cost*
Chapter 10: *The Plan*
Chapter 11: *The Fight Within*
Chapter 12: *A Family Affair*
Chapter 13: *Awakening*
Chapter 14: *Who's next*
Epilogue
Thank You

Prologue

After the global devastation of the last world war, Earth was left in ruins. Once-magnificent cityscapes were turned into mountains of twisted rubble and ash. The natural beauty of thriving forests, plush open fields, rich valleys, and even the frozen tundra, fell prey to the heart-wrenching languages of war and the harsh bloodshed of battle. At the apex, cities and civilizations were erased by the exchange of nuclear pleasantries, driving throngs of people into enormous underground city shelters and bunkers

Nations, cultures, and modern advancements were lost as more and more people fled to the safety of the underground bunkers. Some with affluence and access to books and other small items that could be carried took them below. Many of those who were able to bring knowledge with them chose to share what they had, while others only passed it on to a select few within their underground circle.

With each passing generation, old prejudices faded, building emotional bridges that united the subtle differences of humanity and spawned melting pots of new cultures, societies, and nations within the various different bunkers. As a result, unique languages and cultures blossomed from the melding of societies.

People used their knowledge to form councils and committees to rule over their communities, governing justly. And though life was peaceful for most, it was far from perfect. In some bunkers, human nature couldn't help but crave power. Different families used their knowledge of the old world to place themselves in positions of power and strength, forming kingdoms and other provinces.

The people, however, grew weary of their current situations, and similar to humanity of old, these unique ecosystems couldn't resist their own human need to explore the forgotten world above or to expand their empires. Once people began resurfacing, they found that without humanity getting in nature's way, the earth was able to heal itself and thrive like never before. Unpredictable flora grew wild and unimaginable fauna roamed this boundless, mythical new Earth.

Humanity vowed to learn from their ancestors' mistakes and left the earth as it was. In harmony with the earth, wonderful new technologies and innovations sprung to life to move some nations and kingdoms forward. They built cities which flowed and moved with the beauty of the land instead of plowing through it. Large structures melded with nature.

But not all agreed with technology. Other regions and provinces shied away from technology, choosing to stay close to their traditions of the natural laws and grow more attuned with the earth.

As a result of humanity working in tandem with this vast new world, men and women gained extraordinary abilities unheard of before—abilities that helped shape this new world into one where anything and everything can happen.

Chapter 1: *The Message*

The early morning sun peeks out through the cherry blossom trees and smiles over the landscape. In the distance, a babbling brook flows, shaping the valley. Birds sing from the tops of trees as the cherry-blossom leaves flutter in the warm spring breeze.

The morning light shines over Xolani's deep brown skin and rugged facial features as his rich, black hair twists together, reaching towards the sun. Seated cross-legged on the soft grass, Xolani closes his eyes and tilts his head back, taking in slow, steady breaths. His hands rest comfortably on the plush grass cushioning him while he meditates.

He forces himself to focus, but the cushy ground beneath him turns hard, and a cold chill replaces the warmth of the spring breeze on Xolani's face. The peaceful sounds of nature have been replaced with an unsettling silence that grows increasingly louder. He grimaces as he opens his eyes to flickering street lights coursing down a dark, empty street. The dim, erratic flow of light outlines partially demolished buildings. Xolani's brow instinctively lowers as he rises to his feet, turning his body at an angle as he moves forward with caution to examine his new surroundings. Misty rain cascades over him, building to a steady downpour. The rain soaks through his clothes, making his shirt cling to his sculpted body. Though water floods down his face and distorts his vision, he can still make out a shadowy figure hiding in the darkness. Inching towards it, he reaches out to the figure, waiting for his eyes to adjust to the darkness. He feels for the shadowy figure but a gaping hole in a dilapidated building has taken its place.

Xolani breathes in deeply before creeping into the open wound of the building. Only then does he exhale. Water still trickles down his face as he examines the half-gutted room. The flickering streetlight reflects on an old picture frame across the room, and Xolani moves to pick it up.

The glass is severely cracked, but he peers past the cracks at the teenagers—a set of male twins laughing with two girls. A grin plays on his lips before a flood of long-forgotten memories induce waves of repressed hatred. Xolani quickly looks away and inhales deeply.

"Enough!" he snaps.

"The time draws near, Xolani," a dark voice whispers, reverberating all around him.

Feeling trapped, Xolani tries to take a breath, but it catches in his throat. The picture frame slips from his grasp, the sound of the glass shattering echoes through the room. Bracing for an attack, Xolani glances around the room to locate the source of the sinister voice. His heart pounding in his ears, he steps back into the street.

"Show yourself!" His voice echoes over the cascade of heavy rain, but the scuffling of his wet shoes on the pavement drowns out his voice. The hair at the back of his neck stands on end—he can feel eyes watching his every move.

From behind him, the hot breath of the dark voice whispers into Xolani's ear, "Your time is up."

Swiveling, Xolani blasts fire from his left hand and water from his right, only for both elements to disperse into the empty street.

"Show yourself!"

Inaudible whispers fill the air, growing louder and louder. Intent on locating the origin of the whispers, he doesn't notice the street liquifying beneath him. Too late, he tries to balance but slowly starts to sink. With every tug and every movement Xolani makes, he sinks deeper into the street.

"Daddy!" the voices of Xolani's two children grab his attention as they yell for help from behind him. He struggles to turn and break free but to no avail—the liquified street continues to pull him further down.

"Daddy, help us! Daddy!" The terrified cries for help pound at his eardrums.

"I'm coming, I'm coming!" Xolani yells, struggling with all his might to break free. But every move makes him sink deeper into the street.

"Xolani! Save the kids, just save the kids, the kids."

Xolani turns his head to see his wife, Raine, beside him, panic clear on her face as she sinks deeper and deeper into the street next to him.

Xolani extends his arms to an out-of-reach Raine. His hands tremble in horror as Raine descends into the black abyss. Blood rushes through his skull, blurring his vision, his breath coming out in short gasps as Xolani struggles to free himself.

"Raine! I'm here! Hold on!" His voice cracks as he frantically shoots fire and water from his hands to move the blackened earth from around him. Tears fill his eyes as the street pulls him down at an alarming rate. Fire, water, and chunks of the street fly through the air as he tries to escape the liquefied tomb to save his family. The sound of the children and Raine screaming for him fills his mind as he continues to descend into the tar-filled blackness. The pressure increases around his chest, causing the air to gradually leave his lungs.

"Daddy?" a soft voice says before Xolani feels a hand on his shoulder. He opens his eyes and falls forward, gasping for air. Slowly, he realizes that he is in the Cherry Blossom Forest. Kneeling beside him is Niya, his twelve-year-old daughter.

Her two long braids of thick, dark brown hair fall forward, and with a flip of her hand, she quickly tosses them behind her. Pointy pink clips that match the semi-pink circular frames keep her braids fastened. Two smaller braids flow down in front of her ears. Her green eyes and cute button nose complement her brown skin.

She looks down at her father, her brow furrowed. "Daddy, are you okay? I felt your light, but it was different." Niya's voice belies her concern.

In an attempt to ease his daughter's concern, Xolani smiles. "Yes, I'm fine baby, just deep in meditation." But he doesn't meet her eyes as he rises to his feet, afraid she'd see his fear.

"Mommy was calling for you. She's about to leave for the market, I think. I'm sure she just wants to let you know."

Xolani motions to her and they begin the trek toward their cabin at the base of the snow-topped Mount Eternest.

6

"Daddy, are you sure you're okay?" The words explode from her mouth, and Xolani nearly jumps out of his skin at the loud volume of her voice.

"You don't look well," she says.

"I'm fine, promise. My ears aren't. But I'm fine. It was just some mental conditioning—a little mental sparring. I might have been a little too hard on myself, that's all."

"Come on, Daddy. Mental sparring? I think you make this stuff up to make us think you're smart," Niya jokes.

"It's a real thing. You know how to visualize what you want or to see yourself achieving a certain goal, right?"

"Yes," Niya answers

"Mental sparring is similar to visualizing a goal. The difference is that you are constantly thinking of contingencies for things that might happen. It's mostly used to prepare for different combat scenarios."

Only knowing her father as a man of peace, Niya stops herself from laughing. The mere thought of her father preparing to fight someone let alone fighting anyone, was comical. He was too gentle a man

"Are you getting ready for a fight, Daddy?"

Xolani gives her a loving smile. "It's always better to be a warrior in a garden than a gardener in a war."

"Daaadddy."

"Niiyya."

"Why do you *never* answer questions?"

"Why do you *never* speak as if you are talking with your father?"

"Because my father raised me to be me and not who others wished I'd be," Niya retorts.

A smile plays on Xolani's lips as he chuckles and hugs Niya. "That is very, very true, my star. Don't you ever forget that," he says as they continue walking. Woodland creatures near the tree line shuffle and scurry along serenading their stroll.

"What are you getting Keon for his Dynamism Day?" Niya asks with a tilt of her head and a smile.

Xolani glances down, his hand poised behind his back. "Your brother likes things, doesn't he? I'm sure your mother and I will get him . . . something or other."

"Really, Daddy?" she says with a slight playful annoyance. Niya emphasizes her words with a sassy motion of her head. "Of course, whatever you give him will be a something or other. I figured that."

"Then why'd you'd ask?" Xolani says with a smirk.

"Daddy?!"

"Why do you ask?" Xolani says as he notices the ulterior motive hiding behind Niya's deceivingly innocent face, "His Dynamism Day is still a few days away. Be honest, you're hoping I cook my famous seitan sausage balls, aren't you?" He gently nudges his arm against hers.

"Yep, that's it," she replies, though her nose wrinkled at the thought. "But really, I'm just curious, I guess . . . I mean, I see the townspeople making a big deal out of it, and I know it's important for everyone to celebrate their own Dynamism Day by cooking their favorite foods and playing their favorite games, but I was wondering why do *we* celebrate it?"

"We celebrate it to show gratitude for what the Creator has given us, specifically our gifts. And everyone's actual Dynamism Day can be different. With it often being celebrated on the birth day of that child's ninth birth year . . . Our gifts are presents from the Creator, unique to each individual person. Genetics does play a part in what gifts people have, but even if two people have similar gifts, those two people will not use their gifts in the same way. Of course, not everyone receives a gift, let alone multiple gifts by the day of their Dynamism—"

"I understand the concept of the ceremony, Daddy, and all the other stuff. In a few days, we will, hopefully, be celebrating Keon's new abilities"—catching the stern look from Xolani, Niya corrects herself—"the gifts Keon will have or will possibly be getting. I get that completely, but what's the point of celebrating something you may or may not get, if we can't use it? I mean, you and Mommy have multiple gifts and—"

"As do you," Xolani interjects.

"You say our abilities are gifts, but how can it be a gift if we can't share it with others?"

"It saddens me to hear you feel this way." Xolani places a hand on Niya's shoulder, bringing them both to a halt. "The things we can do . . . Your abilities are gifts. Never feel any other way about them. One day, my star, you will see. However, right now . . ." He sighs. "I get it, when you go into town and see others using their gifts, it's frustrating, I can't say I fully understand how that makes you feel." They continue walking toward the cabin. "When I was your age, I got to play and use my gifts openly, but, Niya, please listen to me. It is very important that we never show anyone outside our family what we can do. Your mother and I don't use our gifts outside of the valley. And we expect you to do the same. One day, I promise, I will explain everything to you. But for now, please trust me. Okay?"

"Okay," Niya mumbles, her voice tinged with sadness and her shoulders slumped.

Xolani stops and turns to her, gently cupping and lifting her chin.

"I see you, my star," he says in a soothing tone.

"I see you too, Daddy," Niya says in the same soothing tone before they continue on.

"Do you know where your brother went?" Xolani asks. "He managed to make it out of the house before me this morning."

"He's by the creek somewhere with Miss Lupita. Last night, he couldn't stop talking about some big experiment they're doing today."

"Interesting. I wonder what she's up to now?"

"I don't know. Miss Lupita is weird."

Xolani chuckles. "Why do you say she's weird?"

Niya shrugs. "I don't know. She's just weird."

"She's different, yes, but that doesn't make her weird."

"No, her being weird makes her weird."

"Is that how we describe people, by calling them names?"

"No, sir," Niya replies.

Xolani puts his arm around her and pulls her closer to his side. "We are all different. Just because she doesn't fit into our idea of normal doesn't make her weird." He pauses for a moment before saying, "Can you go see what concoction they're cooking up? And make sure you and your brother get in a sparring match or two before lunch."

Niya shoots him a disapproving look. "Do we have to?"

"Yes, my star, you do."

"Okay," she says with a grumble. "Hey, Daddy, how come you never use all your gifts when we spar?"

"I feel my water and air gifts are enough to handle you," he jokes before adding in a more serious tone, "My fire and earth gifts can be more lethal than my others. Long ago, I learned that every tool at my disposal may not be the right one. Now, hurry up. If you don't get going, you might miss one of Miss Lupita's amazing experiments. It's good to show interest in what your brother likes, and you both need your exercise."

Niya grabs one of her braids and twists it through her fingers, sighing heavily. "Why do we need to practice? We aren't even supposed to use our gifts."

"You can use your gifts," Xolani replies. "Just not around strangers. Now, be sure to walk. Do not, I repeat, do not teleport. Miss Lupita has told me how you pop in and scare her from time to time."

Niya rolls her eyes at her father before walking away. Xolani stands there for a moment watching her. Niya turns, displaying a wide grin with a mischievous glint in her eye, then she vanishes out of sight.

"That kid will be the death of me," Xolani mutters, shaking his head in disapproval as he turns in the direction of the cabin and continues his trek. Once he reaches the front door, he opens it and is greeted by the lingering smell of breakfast. His rumbling stomach reminds him to eat as the thoughts of fresh apple butter and jelly spread over warm toast make his mouth salivate. The sound of his wife's alluring voice humming from the kitchen distracts his stomach from all thoughts of food. He's captivated and follows her voice to the kitchen. Xolani stops at the entryway. Then leans against the doorframe of the kitchen to admire his love as she moves around, cleaning the remnants of a once-dirty kitchen.

Sunlight radiates off Raine's peachy skin as she wipes off the counter. A cascade of sunlight flowing down her perfectly messy auburn hair catches his attention as he steps into the kitchen. Xolani grabs a piece of seitan sausage from a plate on the table and quickly stuffs it in his mouth. Once he has swallowed the sausage, he walks up behind his wife and wraps his arms around her waist, relishing the warmth of her body against his.

"Good morning, my moon," he says. "Thank you for cooking breakfast this morning. It smells wonderful. I would have cleaned the mess."

Raine leans back into the embrace and rubs a hand over Xolani's arm. "I know, my love." Setting the cloth down on the counter, she turns to face him. "But I was already in here."

He winks at her. "You are truly amazing."

"I know." Raine chuckles.

He lowers his head and kisses her, amazed at how each kiss they shared still felt like the first.

After a moment, Raine pulls away, but her arms remain wrapped around him. "That was a welcome surprise. Is there more?" she asks with a grin.

"There is always more for you." With that, he lowers his lips to hers again, but after a brief kiss, he pulls away abruptly.

The joy drains from his face and his voice is tinged with worry when he asks, "Can you feel Keon with Lupita?"

Raine frowns. "That's where he said he was going when he rushed out of here this morning. I'll check." She closes her eyes for a brief moment, then opens them again. "Yep, he's with her. Is something wrong?"

Xolani turns his gaze away from her. "Nothing . . . well, this morning someone was able to project their will into my mind, causing my consciousness to be taken elsewhere."

"How? I thought you learned to block mental persuasion?" Raine asks in disbelief.

"I did, from some of the greatest scholars alive. But, somehow, I was still vulnerable. If Niya hadn't sensed its light and touched me, I might have still been trapped."

Worry clouds Raine's eyes. "Could it have been Niya? I mean, she's not in full control of her gifts yet, but who else could it have been? We are miles from anyone else. Well, except for Lupita, but she's not telepathic."

"Not that we know of. Niya's gifts are greater than she knows and possibly greater than we know, but it wasn't her. However, Niya's insight on an energy similar to mine makes me wonder if it was Xaden or someone who knows the details of his death."

"But how? No one knows about that night, except you, me, your old friend Rashid, and your father."

Xolani cuts his eyes at her as she continues, "And he's not talking. Plus, it couldn't have been Xaden. The U.R.A made resurrections illegal decades ago."

"We both know the United Regime Assembly has a nice idea of what world harmony can look like, but no one listens to those pompous windbags." Xolani gestures with his hands as he starts to rant. "They only suggest change and make superficial laws that don't even matter to their own individual countries, let alone the rest of the world. They don't have any real say or influence in the world." He sighs and rubs a hand over his face. "But I digress. I've replayed that night in my mind for years. Can you honestly say he's dead? Because I can't. In the chaos of the fight, did either of us really have time to assess the end result as we fled? Either way, there are stranger things in this world than a resurrection. Whoever was in my head this morning made sure I knew the time is near."

"What do you mean?" Raine asks.

"I don't know, but it's not good. I don't know if Xaden survived, or who would want to bring up the past, but I think we can both agree this isn't the end."

"Should we have Lupita take the kids and—" Raine's words get cut off at a loud knock at the front door.

"I'll get it," Xolani says, gently pushing his wife behind him.

"You don't think it's—"

"Doesn't matter what I think, we're about to find out." Xolani heads to the door with Raine following close behind him. Suddenly, she grabs his arm, stopping him in his tracks.

"Xolani, I've lost my connection to the kids. I'm unable to feel them or their location."

"I'll distract whomever it is. Send Niya a telepathic message. Lupita will know what to do if necessary." Another knock burst from the door. Xolani grabs Raine by the shoulders. "No matter what, I see you."

She smiles briefly as she says, "I see you, too."

Releasing a breath through his nose, Xolani reaches for the door and slowly opens it.

A tall, slender man, appearing not to be a day over seventeen, stands at attention, his back as straight as a rod. The only thing straighter than his posture is his short black hair, cut in military-style. His gaudy purple-and-gold military uniform is stiffly starched. Wide, hazel-blue eyes narrow at the ends, accentuating the small scar over his right eyebrow and his slightly crooked nose—the only imperfections on his otherwise youthful almond-colored face.

"May we help you?" Raine asks.

The tall man pulls out a scroll and inhales deeply, before his nervous squeaky voice is heard. "Are you"—he clears his throat—"the Ravenesses?"

"Depends on who's asking," Xolani replies.

"I am Gibbon, the Nuhana royal messenger. By the royal order of King Xerxes, Xolani and Raine Raveness are invited for an audience of the utmost importance. There is an urgent royal matter the king must discuss with them. The king requests that they appear before him in the high court *immediately*. It is of grave importance they come with me as soon as possible. Please tell me, are you Xolani and Raine Raveness?"

"Gibbon, any urgent or important matter of Nuhana is Nuhana's concern, not ours. The crown and those who serve it have no authority here. This is Aberrant territory. The king has no dominion here."

"King Xerxes said Xolani would respond in this manner and to give him this," Gibbon says, reaching into his coat pocket with fumbling hands. He pulls out a letter and hands it to Xolani. The letter is sealed with purple wax and stamped with a roaring lion—the royal Uwani family seal.

Xolani opens the letter, turning it slightly so Raine can read along with him. After a few moments, they look up at each other and try to mask their worry. Xolani searches his mind for ways to get out of the request but sees no other choice than to comply. Resting his hands on Raine's shoulders, he looks intently into her eyes. There's a heaviness in his voice when he says, "Let's gather some clothes for the trip."

"No need, sir, all will be provided. Please come with me," Gibbon interjects.

Exchanging a glance, Xolani and Raine follow Gibbon outside to a luxurious royal black car with tinted windows and clean kept tires.

"It's not a short trip to Nuhana," Raine says. "I'm sure King Xerxes wouldn't know if we took a few minutes so I can use the bathroom."

Gibbon fiddled with the buttons on his uniform coat, his eyes downcast. "My car is equipped with the latest sky conversion." He hesitates. "So, it shouldn't be too terrible of a ride . . . but the skyway traffic could be an issue. I'm sure it wouldn't hurt for us to take a *few* more minutes."

"Thank you." Raine curtseys playfully before hurrying into the cabin.

An awkward silence descends between the men as they wait for Raine. Gibbon ceases his fiddling and instead holds his left elbow with his right hand, rocking back and forth as he eyes the cabin's front door. Minutes seem to drag, the silence growing increasingly louder.

"Did you happen to catch the Hill Battle last night on the feed?" Gibbon asks.

14

"No, we don't own a television to watch Hill Battles or any other sporting events," Xolani says bluntly.

"Oh, you really missed a great match," Gibbon says in a rush. "Victor Bow dominated the hill yet again. No other challenger came close to taking him down. He is still the undefeated king of Hill Battle. I think he's going to go all the way to the Grand Mountain Championship this year, or at least to the quarter- or even semi-finals."

"I don't follow sports. I'd rather stimulate my mind with a good book."

"Oh, I don't, either. I just heard it on the Intelligence Report this morning." He pauses briefly to take a breath. "I know I shouldn't watch that garbage—it's all recycled nonsense and who knows who's subjective point of view it's from—but it's addictive. I mean, look at the leader of Amerigo, you never know what that guy is going to say or even do next. I mean really—"

"We *don't* have to talk," Xolani mutters.

Gibbon's mouth opens and closes like a fish seeking air, then he looks to the ground. A deafening quiet lingers between them, with only the sound of birds chirping in the blossom trees and the flowing river breaking the silence.

Finally, Raine bursts out of the cabin and flashes a smile at the men. "Whew, I feel better. Didn't want to hold that the whole way."

Xolani locks eyes with her, and in a calm voice, he says, "Glad you feel better. Did you check the stove and the two candles while you were inside?"

"I did. We don't need to worry. The stove and candles are out."

Xolani smiles at Raine's response. "Good. Well then, off we go to see the king."

When they reach the car, Xolani opens the door for Raine, then looks back to the spot where he saw Niya vanish before getting in after Raine. Gibbon inserts the key into the ignition and twists to start the car's engine. As the engine comes to life, Gibbon turns a dial and the car begins to hover.

The tires extend out slightly as they angle downward, parallel with the ground. The car's engine hums as it inches forward slightly. Then, with a sudden roar of power, the car rockets into the sky and fades out of sight.

Chapter 2: *Miss Lupita*

Niya looks at her father before turning and walking away. She can feel her father's eyes on her as she walks.

"And no telepathy or telekinesis of any kind!"

She turns back around with a twinkle of mischief in her eyes. Grinning wide at her father, she vanishes on the spot, and reappears behind a cherry blossom tree several yards away from their cabin. Her father approaches the cabin and enters. Once he's out of view, she hunches over and places her hands on her head.

Okay, you can do this, Niya. Just picture Dad inside our cabin. He's walking through the hall until he finds Mom . . . who's probably still cleaning the kitchen.

She inhales deeply and exhales slowly as she quiets her thoughts. Images of Raine and Xolani conversing in the kitchen begin to fill her mind and chunks of their conversation break through the static.

"Wait, who else could've been in Dad's mind? . . . I can too control my gifts . . . Miss Lupita? That crazy lady protect us? Okay . . . What, who's Xaden?"

The soft hum of a flying vehicle passes overhead, breaking Niya's focus. She opens her eyes to see a car flying in the sky before it lands in front of the cabin. She peeks out from behind the tree as a man steps out of the car and straightens his clothes.

Who's this? Xaden, maybe? The car has the Uwani royal seal on it. Is the Xaden guy royalty?

Niya stops speculating as the man walks to the door and raises his fist to knock but stops himself. He turns around to take a few steps back to his car and begins to mumble.

Is he talking to himself? Niya wonders, laughing quietly to herself. The man frantically shakes his hands, his chest rising and falling with every deep breath he takes. Finally, he stops shaking his hands and heads back to the door. He knocks, then steps back. After a few moments, he knocks again.

Mom and Dad are in there, what's taking them so—oh, there they are.

Niya glances around for a closer spot to teleport to, but there's nowhere that would keep her hidden from sight. Biting on her lip, she closes her eyes and clears her mind, trying to focus in on what they were saying. The silence of her own thoughts fills her head. She takes in a deep breath and exhales, then tries again, but silence persists in her mind.

Why can't I hear them? They're right there.

Perhaps she simply wasn't using her gifts correctly. Sighing, she opens her eyes, only to find that her mother wasn't outside anymore.

She frowns. *"Where did Mom go? How did I not—"*

"Niya!" Raine's voice booms in Niya's mind, interrupting her thoughts. "Can you hear me?"

"I can hear you, you don't have to yell," Niya replies. "My head is not a Comm-D you can just dial into, you know?"

"Niya!"

"Sorry," she whines. "Where did you go? You're not in front of the cabin anymore."

"I'm inside . . . Niya! Are you spying on us again?"

"No. Yes. Maybe, just a little," Niya answers sheepishly.

"We'll discuss this later. But now, I need you to tell Miss Lupita to take you and your brother home."

"Take us home? I don't understand. We are home."

"Niya, please. Miss Lupita will know what to do. Just give her the message to take you and your brother home. Remember, I see you and your brother. Now go!"

"I see you, Mommy," Niya says before vanishing and reappearing next to a small cottage. She stands there, listening to the sound of the creek trickling behind her and bites her lip. She fights the urge building inside her to run and look for Miss Lupita and Keon. The gentle breeze flows over her, the warm sun kissing her face. Birds chirping nearby fill the air as her impatience eats away at her.

KABOOM! A loud explosion goes off in the distance.

"There!" Niya exclaims, then vanishes to reappear between Miss Lupita and Keon.

"Niya! You frightened me, child," Miss Lupita says in a startled voice as she runs her hands through her straight, grayish-black hair. She is a small, petite woman with pale skin, her wrinkled face showing the many years of a hard but joyful life. Miss Lupita brushes off her earthly green gown to recompose herself.

"Mom and Dad are—"

"Don't be rude, child. Your father would be furious if he knew you were scaring me again," Miss Lupita says as she continues to lecture. "After all, I'm such a frail old lady. Why would you want to give my heart such a fright? But I digress, we are in the middle of a lesson, so—"

"But—"

"No butts, hands, or any other body part you might want to interject."

Niya shakes her head and lets out a long, low sigh, as she remains quiet.

"Now, as I was saying . . . what was I saying?" Frowning, Miss Lupita scratches her head.

"Miss Lupita, don't you remember?" Keon's green eyes sparkle with anticipation, his face and blond mohawk covered with dirt from the earlier blast. "You were explaining the chemical reaction that caused the explosion."

Miss Lupita nods. "Right, yes. Exactly. See, a little hydrogen with a bit of chlorine, a lot of pressure and a fuse can—"

"Miss Lupita! Are you teaching Keon to blow things up?"

"Of course not, I'm teaching him how to make an explosion that will blow things up. Two totally different things." The woman smiles as Niya smacks her forehead in frustration.

"Mom and Dad were taken by some royal guy named Xaden. We have to go and help them."

20

"Xaden?" Fear and worry, flashed through Miss Lupita's light blue eyes that often washed over a person as her soft, inviting smile fills you with a sense of peace. "How do you know that name? Were you being nosey again?"

"Yes, but that's not important. Mom and Dad were taken."

"Taken where?"

"I don't know."

"Were they forced to leave?

"Well, I don't think so, but I know they didn't want to go. Come on, we're wasting time."

"Okay, tell me exactly what happened?"

"Mom and Dad were talking about a vision Dad had, about a guy named Xaden."

"Are you sure?"

"Yes, then he—"

"He who?" Miss Lupita snaps.

"Xaden! He knocks on the door. They talk, then Mom steps away and yells in my head to tell you to take us home, then she and—"

Miss Lupita grabs Niya's wildly gesturing arms. "What exactly did she say?"

"Just to tell you to take Keon and me home."

Miss Lupita looks down and releases Niya before she starts to pace. Her face grows heavy as it displays the weight of the responsibility that is now placed on her shoulders. Closing her eyes, she lifts her head to the sky and places her hands together, murmuring a prayer. She then smiles a playful grin as she kneels, placing a hand on the loose soil from the explosion. With tilted heads and raised brows, the children watch the soil inch together. Rocks shift together as they ascend to the surface. Sticks and twigs slither in with the rocks. Keon and Niya stand and watch in awe and surprise as the soil, rocks, and sticks twist and slowly meld together to form a carriage. Miss Lupita picks up a handful of dirt and molds it in her hands. As the kids look on in astonishment, she morphs the dirt into a sparrow and leans in close to the newly formed creature as she whispers to it. Then, in one swift motion, she tosses the sparrow into the air. Gracefully, it takes flight, soaring off into the distance.

Miss Lupita searches around until she spots her target and hurries towards the creek. At the creek bed, she stops and stares into the water.

Keon and Niya stand at the carriage, giving each other pointed looks. What is Miss Lupita doing now? At this point in their lives, they know it's better and usually more fun to watch her work than have her explain her actions. However, this time, the kids were caught unaware to Miss Lupita's gifts.

"Miss Lupita, how did you . . . I mean, I thought you didn't have gifts?" Niya asks with curiosity and a touch of bluntness in her voice.

"My child, you've never seen me use them, and so you assumed I had none," Miss Lupita replies, though she remains focused on the flowing water.

"I just thought, well . . ." Niya fumbles to find the right words.

"I didn't get my gift at my Dynamism. In fact, it was many years later before I found my gift."

"Like me?" Keon exclaims.

"Not exactly," Miss Lupita says. "You're still at the age where your gifts will manifest themselves naturally. I, on the other hand, spent years developing what eventually became my gift."

"I thought the creator doesn't give gifts after we've reached our Dynamism day?" Niya asks.

"Child, you have so much to learn. Your Dynamism day is not the day the creator gives you gifts. Those gifts have been inside you since your conception. As we grow, our gifts are presents we need to unwrap. Sadly, many don't. The way I see it, you can become one of two types of people. A person who can, or a person who does. Both have the potential, but only one acts on the belief that they already have the ability. The choice is"—Miss Lupita quickly stabs her hands into the water to pull out two frantic golden fish—"yours. Gotcha!"

22

Niya and Keon lean forward and look on in wide-eyed wonder as the fish wiggle and begin to elongate—their fins stretching into horse legs as their mouths and tails slowly catch up to form the rest of their newly formed horse bodies. The golden-brown horses lie kicking and neighing in the rushing water and attempt to swim like fish.

"Fish! Focus." Though it's a command, her voice is warm and understanding as she places her hands on them. Their postures relax, and after a moment, they rise to walk out of the water. "I know I've disrupted your life and I do apologize," Miss Lupita says to the confused fish-turned-horses. "I beg a favor. I need to take these children home to keep them safe. Will you two please pull our carriage?"

The horses tilt their heads slightly before looking at one another. After a moment's deliberation, they look back to Miss Lupita and neigh before nodding their heads.

"Thank you, my friends." She leads them over to the carriage and places the reins on them. "Once we've finished our journey, if you choose, I will return you to your former state. I think we should call you with the shorter mane Fransisco, and you with the longer mane Francine."

"How do you know she's a she and he's a he?" Keon asks.

"I'm sure your parents would love to have that talk with you," Miss Lupita says quickly, "but let us go, our chariot awaits."

"Do we have to take that?" Niya points to the carriage, disgust in her voice. "Couldn't you have made a car?"

"Our journey requires stealth, not speed or extravagance," Miss Lupita says in a loving tone. "Where we're going, a nice buggy will fit in nicely. Come along, children." She nudges them forward. "We have a long way to go."

"Where are we going?" Keon and Niya asks almost simultaneously.

"Home."

Chapter 3: *The Prodigal One*

Leaving the skyways, Gibbon, Raine, and Xolani descend from the clouds. Nuhana, a harmonious blend of technology and nature, fills the landscape. The gorgeous, natural metropolis intertwines with an urban forest, its perimeter protected by an enormous metal outer wall. In the middle of it all sits the royal tree palace, a gargantuan tree which dwarfs the entire city. An earthy wall of boulders and moss protects the palace.

"Vehicle RFV-4," a stern voice announces over the car's radio as they approach. "You are not cleared to fly in restricted air space. Change your flight path or be shot down."

Gibbon grimaces, shaking his head slightly as he fumbles with the car's console.

"Gibbon? What's going on?" Raine asks as Gibbon continues looking through the console.

"Nothing" Gibbon replies with an uneasiness to his voice. "Just standard—"

BOOM!

BOOM!

"—procedure."

Explosions near the sides of the car illuminate the urgency of the situation as two sleek aircrafts appear and align their sights on the flying vehicle. Gibbon quickly grabs the steering wheel and focuses on flying.

"Nothing?!" Raine shouts at Gibbon as she peers out the window. "This is not nothing. This is planes shooting at us!"

Gibbon keeps his focus as he maneuvers through the tops of Nuhana. He does his best to keep the city structures between them and the CF-2s.

"Isn't there some type of access code or secret word you're supposed to give them? Preferably before they shoot us down," Xolani hangs on to the car's grip handle as his words are drowned out by the deafening boom of explosions ringing all around them.

Raine and Xolani sway with the pull of the car's force as Gibbon expertly maneuvers around the city structures to stay ahead of the CF-2s. In the distance, a purple landing pad comes into view atop the royal tree palace. An outline of a roaring lion trimmed in gold can be seen as they speed closer.

"Oh, how stupid of me," Gibbon blurts, "I forgot to radio in the access code before flying into Nuhana airspace" as he presses a combination of buttons on the front console. "Tower, this is RFV-4. Requesting permission to land on royal platform one. Access code purple, G-M-R-W-1." The sound of radio static fills the car before the CF-2s cease firing and depart.

"Vehicle RFV-4, permission granted. Proceed to royal platform one."

"Oh, thank the Creator," Raine says gratefully, throwing her hands up.

Gibbon, fully confident in his impending landing, steers toward the royal platform with the roaring lion.

"Any landing you can walk away from is a good one. And this will be a great one," Gibbon says as he releases a lever to his left before pulling back on the steering wheel, causing Raine and Xolani to be tossed back into their seats as the car shifts, speeds, and lowers onto the landing pad. They hover just enough for the tires to revert back to their original state, then lower gently down.

"Here we are," Gibbon states as he pulls up the lever, then releases his seatbelt. "Safe and sound." He turns to face Raine and Xolani. "Let's go meet the king."

Xolani and Raine stare at him, not knowing whether to be grateful to be alive or murder him for almost killing them.

"Gibbon, that was some excellent flying, but next time . . ." Xolani says with a gentleness in his voice after exhaling deeply. "Could you possibly remember the access code before the near-death experience?"

"I'm sorry about that." Gibbon lowers his head. "This was actually the first time I've flown back into the city, and I just forgot."

"It's okay," Xolani says as he places a hand on Gibbon's shoulder. "I mean, you did almost kill us, but it's fine. For your first time you did amazing, outmaneuvering those fighters like that. How'd you learn to fly?"

Gibbon clears his throat, his face flushing. "Most nights, after my duties, I use the flight simulator. There's not much else for me to do, so I do that."

"That seemed like a little more than time behind a simulator." Xolani tilts his head toward Gibbon, who's fiddling with his shirt sleeve.

"In all honesty, sir, I want to be a pilot, but . . ."

"But?" Xolani asks encouragingly.

"The officers don't take me seriously." Gibbon's voice rises, his nostrils flaring. "They don't want a ground rat like me flying. They tell me to stay in the trash where I belong . . . So, I practice in the simulators at night, every night when no one else is there."

"No one should have to put up with such nonsense," Raine says in a gentle tone. Xolani smiles and nods in agreement. "You have rights and should take action."

"Too . . . too many politics," Gibbon mumbles. "I could never, besides, we really need to get inside, we shouldn't keep King Xerxes waiting any longer."

"Yes, of course," Xolani says. "However, do you think we could freshen up before meeting the king?"

"Um, well, I don't know. I mean, we really shouldn't delay any further," Gibbon says.

"It was a very long sky ride. I'd hate to meet the king in these tattered old things I wear around the house," Raine adds.

Gibbon breaks eye contact with Raine and Xolani, staring into nothingness for a long while. He turns and mutters his options under his breath.

"It didn't feel like our ride was that long, forty, maybe fifty minutes tops," he mutters as he swivels back to face them. "King Xerxes commanded you be brought directly to him with no detours or stops,"

"Gibbon," Xolani persists, "I bet when you met the king—"

"I've never met the king." Gibbon flushes bright red as the whisper falls from his lips.

"Never?" Raine and Xolani say in unison, both wearing similar expressions of shock.

"I've been in his presence," Gibbon mutters. "But I've never *officially* met him."

"Then you must understand. Give us five, ten minutes at the most. A quick shower, fresh clothing, and we'll be off to see the king. I swear. After all, you said everything will be provided for us."

"Okay." Gibbon heaves out a sigh. "Ten minutes, but that's all. I'll take you to the closest guest quarters, so you can shower and change. And after that, straight to the king!"

Xolani nods. "Of course, straight to the king."

With that, they exit the car and follow Gibbon. Once inside, Gibbon leads them down a long corridor. Their footsteps on the gray marble floor echo through the hall as they walk. Every few meters, the hall branches off, but they continue straight. The gold trim from the landing pad continues inside to the top and bottom of the bare lavender walls. Studying the empty wall, Raine realizes the color of the walls are changing into various shades of purple.

"Xolani, are you seeing this? The walls are fading from one shade of purple to another."

"It's the Mother Tree," Xolani replies. "The royal palace was built inside her."

Raine stops to examine the wall, her eyebrows rising as she focuses on the wall. "I've read about the Mother Tree but never thought I'd get to see it—let alone be in it."

"Yes, the Mother Tree is quite impressive," Gibbon pipes up. "She is the center of Nuhana." He turns to find Raine several feet behind them, still examining the wall. He taps Xolani, who stops and turns.

"I've read that the Mother Tree was some sort of historical data base and that our ancestors would learn and share knowledge through her network of roots. Is it true that she is connected to everything? And anyone that touches her will know what she knows?" Raine asks.

"Not exactly. Things have gotten a little embellished over time. Outside of the Royal Uwani family, no one knows how far the Mother Tree's connection goes. However, her reach and depth of knowledge is far and vast. It wouldn't surprise me to learn that she extends as far as, well, across the world to the St. Kenyan Islands or something. But King Xail IV sealed off any and all access to the Mother Tree, the exception being any place on this level. Plain folks like us will probably never know how far her knowledge truly extends." Gibbon trots down the hall again, and they hurry along after him.

Raine tilts her head. "Why this level?"

"Because only members of the Royal Uwani bloodline stay here and are allowed on this level, giving them—and only them—full access to the Mother Tree, as long as they are on this level, that is. We only have access to this level because you are here to see King Xerxes."

"What's stopping us from touching the walls now?" Raine reaches out to touch the wall, but Xolani darts toward her and grabs her hand before she can.

"Don't! It's a transfer of knowledge. Anyone who touches the Mother Tree will learn all she knows as she learns all that you know." He turns to Gibbon. "How much farther? I don't want to make the king wait any longer than he has to."

"Not to worry. We're here." They reach a solid white door wrapped in a golden frame. The words *die verlorenes* are carved on the door. "No one uses this room. I believe it belonged to the royal twins before they died. I'm sure it would be fine for the two of you to freshen up and change inside."

"Are you sure we can use this room?" Raine asks, studying the words carved on the door. "Whatever's scratched on this door seems serious."

"It's ancient Nuhana," Gibbon says. "I think. It says something about *the one is one.* I'm not sure. It's a *very* old language. I'm sure it will be fine. Besides, the two of you will only be using it to change."

"We won't take long. We just need some clothes for after we've freshened up," Xolani says.

"Of course. I just need to inform one of the king's Five that we have arrived. I'll be along with proper clothes. Is there a preference in the type of clothes? Pants? Dress? Tunic?"

"Any clothing will do, Gibbon."

"I will return shortly. Please make yourselves comfortable," Gibbon says as he waves them through the door he's holding open. Stale air hits them as they walk into the room. Dust covers the lavish furniture in the enormous room. The room is split into two similar but unique sides that contain duplicate sets of furniture and bathrooms on opposite sides of the room. On the left is a bedroom set with black-and-gold accents covering everything, on the right, red-and-gold accents.

"Look at this room. Seems someone had an identity issue," Raine says.

Not hearing the humor in his wife's voice, Xolani says, "Or a set of twins."

"Couldn't have guessed that, my love," Raine says with a hint of sarcasm in her tone. She looks over her shoulder to ensure the door was completely closed. "I know you don't care about looking *proper* for the king. Other than fate and pure coincidence, why are we really in your old room?"

"Couldn't have guessed Gibbon would mistakenly put us in my old room, but here we are. We need to be careful what we say and what we ask outside of this room. The Mother Tree records all it hears and feels. Lucky for us, the royal bedrooms are isolated from her."

"My love, you're tense. Let's focus on meeting with the king and going home."

Xolani's eyes widen. "Home! Did Niya understand your message when you called out to her? I tried to reach her during our sky ride and since we've been in the palace. I honestly thought her telepathy would reach my thoughts, but I haven't been successful."

"It was strange even before we left. I had to walk to the end of the cabin before my thoughts finally reached her. I can't seem to reach her now, either. Usually, my empath gifts allow me to feel her general location, but I can't. As a matter of fact, I'm not feeling Keon, you, or anyone else. There's something wrong with my gifts."

"I don't think that's it. There must be some type of dampener designed to block or suppress gifts. I bet there was a smaller version of it in Gibbon's car." Xolani looks around the room, then points to a lamp on the desk closest to Raine. "Touch the metal of that lamp and see if you can absorb its properties."

Raine reaches out and touches the lamp, focusing her attention on it. Her face tightens, and after a moment, she shakes her head.

"I'm completely cut off from the Creator," she hisses. "I can't believe they would design something to hinder our gifts."

"I don't think they specifically designed it for us, more like it was designed for anyone posing a serious threat to the throne, I wonder how that works with the King's Five."

"I don't know," Raine shrugs, "maybe they wear some sort of device or something to protect their gifts from the dampening device."

"Maybe,… but that doesn't matter. You read the letter. King Xerxes knows about our lives and the kids. You know as well as I do that he will hurt them if we don't hear what he wants."

"I know." She sighs. "I thought we'd left this world behind."

Xolani steps closer to Raine and wraps his arms around her.

"Soon, my härt," he murmurs. "We just need to hear out the king, and then we will be on our way."

She lays her head on his chest. "I pray you're right, my liefde."

Wrapped in each other's arms, the world seems to fade away around them.

"I know this seems like an odd question, but what do you think about Gibbon?" Xolani asks.

"He seems okay. Why?"

Xolani shrugs. "I don't know. Just feel bad for the kid, I guess."

"The tin soldier has a heart after all." Raine jabs her husband in the side, her eyes twinkling with humor.

Xolani pulls away from her and pouts. "Is that what I get for sharing my feelings?"

Raine laughs as she lays a hand on his cheek. "I'm just messing with you, my love."

"Xolani, Raine, I have your clothes," Gibbon's nervous voice comes through the door.

Xolani heads to the door and opens it. To his and Raine's surprise, Gibbon is standing in the doorway with a change of clothes under his arm and a fierce-looking woman behind him.

"Um, hello?" Xolani says.

"This is Haygena," Gibbon says. Any trace of joy that was in his voice before has vanished. "She is one of the king's Five and a legionnaire from the Rompeiian Empire of Grétily. She will be taking you to meet King Xerxes."

Haygena plows past Gibbon as she snatches the clothes from him and shoves them at Xolani. "King Xerxes commands you to put these on and come with me. Now!" she snarls.

"Xerxes does not *command* me and *he* is not—"

Before he can say another word, Haygena extends her hand, a pulse of vibrations bursting from her palm. Xolani's feet lift off the floor, and he flies through the air, slamming into the wall.

"Xolani!" Raine shouts, launching forward to blindside Haygena. Xolani struggles to his knees, his chest throbbing from the blast, and raises a hand to stop his wife. Gasping for breath, he looks up at the soldier towering over him.

"No one dishonors the king in my presence! Xerxes is king and commands all. No matter the land you come from, understand?"

"Yeah, I got it," Xolani says as he gets up on his feet. "We will go, not because he is our king, but because we said we would. Do you understand?"

Haygena moves to throw another blow, but Gibbon quickly jumps between them.

"Haygena, I believe great King Xerxes would like to see both Raine and Xolani in one piece, don't you agree?"

Inhaling deeply, Haygena takes a step back. "For once you are correct, Dibbon."

"Gibbon."

Haygena turns all her focus on him, making Gibbon roll his shoulders down to make himself look smaller. He backs up a step. "Gibbon, my name is . . ." His throat bobs at the glare Haygena sent him. "Dibbon is good."

Haygena turns her head to refocus on Xolani. "It is not my place to question King Xerxes, even if he chooses to keep two fugenie in the palace. King Xerxes commands that he meets with you, Xolani, and you alone. The other fugenie must stay here."

Xolani, hearing the slur casually tossed to his love, speaks through slightly clenched teeth as he works to extinguish the sparked rage billowing inside. "My wife and I came to meet with the king. And it *will* be my wife and I that meets with the king."

Sensing the tension, Raine inserts herself between Haygena and Xolani. "My love, it's okay. I'm here, and I'm safe. Please, go meet with Xerxes so we can leave." She places her hand on Xolani's arm and they lock eyes for a moment.

Sighing, because he knows his wife is right, Xolani looks at Haygena. "I need a moment to change. I will be right out."

With untrusting eyes, Haygena points to the far side of the room. "There is a bathroom on either side of this room. I will wait for you to change."

Xolani takes the clothes and walks to the black-and-gold bathroom across the room and shuts the door behind him.

"Are you serious?!" he calls from the bathroom. A moment later, the door opens a sliver and Xolani sticks his head out. "A tunic? I didn't think you would actually bring me a tunic, Gibbon."

"King Xerxes is waiting," Haygena snaps.

Frustrated, Xolani closes the bathroom door. The others hear him grumbling and shuffling until the door opens again. Xolani steps out in a light-green tunic with the royal seal in gold trim on the left chest pocket and hunter-green pants.

Raine and Gibbon cover their mouths in an attempt to hold back their amusement when Xolani tugs at the crotch of his tunic to loosen them. Huffing, Xolani walks to Haygena and motions to leave.

"Stay here with her until given further instructions," Haygena tells Gibbon. "Do not let her out of your sight."

Gibbon nods in obedience as Haygena and Xolani exit into the hallway. The pair walk down the hallway, turning down one hall after another until they reach a hallway vastly bigger than all the rest. The floor in the previous hallways were all marble, but in this hallway it's a bruised metal. Xolani looks down the hall to where an enormous door rests at the end with circular lights glowing from the floor. The lights illuminate two concave pillars in the walls on both sides of the door. .

This isn't where the Five used to stand. I wonder if this is where they go when the king doesn't need them. But I don't see a place for a fifth one to stand?

Haygena whips her arm against Xolani's chest to stop him from moving any further. Xolani's eyes narrow in a glare, but Haygena's attention is solely focused on the enormous doors ahead. She slides her outer leg back, stretching her arms forward, then launches three pulses at the door. As it slowly creaks open, an off-white light breaks through the seams of the enormous heavy doors. Haygena and Xolani stand for a moment until the doors are wide enough to enter King Xerxes' chamber. They step forward, the blinding light engulfing them. With a heavy snap, the doors close behind them.

Chapter 4: *The Journey*

The excitement of riding in an earthy carriage was wearing off. The fact that horses that spontaneously act like fish are drawing the carriage has lost its appeal to Keon and Niya. The children are exhausted from being on the road for hours. The scenic beauty of the countryside blends together in one big blur of boredom.

Lupita glances at the horizon, where the sun is setting over the mountains. They need to find shelter soon. The once carefree and funny teacher has now become an overly cautious protector. As she controls the reins, Keon yawns beside her. He chose to sit next to her with the hope that she would let him control the fish-horses, but as the hours passed, he could see this wasn't going to be that type of trip. Niya, wanting nothing to do with anything about this trip, was sitting inside the carriage, looking up at the sky and wondering where their parents were whisked off to. She continuously tries to reach out to them via telepathy, hoping she'll be able to contact them. For a split second early in the trip, she did. She heard their voices in her mind, clear as day. But just as quickly as she heard them, did they become fleeting whispers that vanished from her mind. Focusing on connecting with them again, she pushes her mind further than she even thought possible. Drilling herself over and over again, using her parents as the incentive to keep going and keep training.

However, the only entertainment for Keon now is to ask Miss Lupita questions. And he only has one question on his mind.

"Miss Lupita, how much *longer*?"

"As long as it takes, my boy, as long as it takes."

"That's what you said the last time."

"If you keep asking the same question, why would you expect a different answer?" Though Miss Lupita answers enthusiastically, he can hear the fatigue in her voice.

Keon shifts in his seat to get a better look at the repetitive countryside crawling past. The beauty of the various reds, oranges, and yellows in the trees escape the youthful mind of an eight-year-old. He gazes out to get lost in his own thoughts. The second he closes his eyes, he remembers Niya is inside the carriage.

"Niya!"

"What? I'm busy. Get out of my head."

"Busy doing what?"

"Nothing for you to worry about."

"Come on, Niya, you can tell me. Doing what?"

"I'm trying to reach Mom and Dad. So, stop using my gifts as a Comm-D and go back to talking to Miss Lupita."

"Sorry, Niya. you're not a Comm-D . . . Can I help?"

"How are you going to help? You don't have gifts and I can do this alone."

"Please. I can hold your hand or help you stay calm or—"

"Keon, stop! You don't have gifts and probably never will. You're useless."

Keon falls silent, then his sister's voice penetrates his mind again.

"Keon . . . I–I didn't mean it. I shouldn't have said that. I'm sure you will get your gifts. I'm sorry, okay?"

"You always have to rub it in that you have gifts and I don't." His anger explodes in his mind. *"But I don't need gifts to be useful. I'm special without them. Even when I get my gifts, I won't use them, because I will be able to do whatever I want without them!"*

Lupita looks down at Keon. His jaw is clenched and tears are trailing down his cheeks.

"Are you okay, Keon?"

At her question, Keon opens his eyes, breaking his mental conversation with Niya.

Wiping the tears from his face, he replies, "Yep, fine."

"You don't look fine. Your face is leaking," Lupita jokes.

"Just talking with Niya."

"Oh, I see. How is she doing alone in the carriage?"

"She's okay. She's looking for Mom and Dad."

Suddenly, Lupita pulls hard on the reins, causing the horses to come to a complete stop. She scrambles off the front seat and into the carriage.

"My child, do not try to contact your parents."

"You told her!" Niya yells, pounding her fist against the carriage wall.

Lupita shakes her head. "Don't be mad at him. He did the right thing by telling me. You shouldn't be opening your mind to find your parents."

"I just want to help them."

"I know you do, and we will. However, there are people out there with gifts like yours who will use your gifts against us if we aren't careful."

"I don't understand. I was only looking for my parents."

"Our minds are like antennas that attract all sorts of energy. Your gifts amplify that. You're capable of reaching vast distances and multitudes of people with your thoughts. But if you aren't careful, reaching out so far is like sending out a beacon for anyone that's listening. Whether your parents or other . . ."

"Other?"

"Yes, other. Come in the front with Keon and me. I'll explain it to both of you."

With a nod, Niya follows Lupita out of the carriage and sits down next to Keon on the front seat.

Grabbing the reins, Lupita gives a quick, hard snap, and Fransisco and Francine trot onward.

"We're not far from Port Ambit," Lupita says after taking in a deep breath. "It's a poor fishing community on the border of the Aberrant territory. People come and go there all the time. No one should think twice of strangers passing through."

"Miss Lupita." Niya heaves a heavy sigh. "Why can't we look for our parents?"

"We're going to Joe's tavern. I'm good friends with the owner. She's one of the kindest, warmest, and most straight-forward people I know. We

38

can stop, eat, get some rest, then continue on in the morning. We'll be safe there."

She falls silent, feeling the children's stares on her. She had no choice but to tell them something. "Years ago, your parents made a series of choices, which are affecting your family now. I know I'm not being very specific about the situation, but I'm sure your parents would rather it come from them and not me."

"If what comes from them?" Keon pipes up.

"If Xaden is the one behind all of this, then I need to get the two of you to a safe place." Her grip on the reins tighten as she makes the decision to tell them more. "Before you were born, Xolani and Raine had to leave Nuhana. Now it seems that they must return."

"Miss Lupita," Niya says in a gentle voice. "Who is Xaden?"

The old woman takes a deep breath and exhales slowly before speaking. "I've never met him, and your parents have never told me anything about him. So, all I know is speculation. However, I will try to state facts and stay away from any untruths. Xaden was one of the princes of Nuhana. The other prince was his twin brother Xalen. Xaden often misused his gifts on the Nuhana people."

"What was his gifts?" Keon asks.

"Teleportation and persuasion."

"Like Niya!"

"How is persuasion a gift?" Niya asks. "What did he do, debate?"

Miss Lupita looks at Niya before answering. "Xaden's ability could make people do anything he wanted them to do."

"Anything?" Keon asks.

"Yes, anything. He'd control people simply by suggesting what he wanted them to do. The good thing was—if you want to see it as a good thing—that he could only control you once. After you were released from his control, he was unable to control you again."

"Miss Lupita, how do you know all this?" Keon asks.

"I've been around, and you tend to hear things when you've been around as long as I have. Xaden was being groomed to be the next Scion, but there was a law that both he and Xalen had claim to be the next Scion. The law also stated that when more than one Scion was present, they had to fight until one submitted and there was one clear winner."

"Why not just let the firstborn of the twins be the Scion?" Niya asks.

"There's no way to tell which one is truly the firstborn once they are older. Either of them could say they were the oldest. Their battle got out of control. Xalen killed Xaden, and their father, King Xerxes, sentenced Xalen to be executed."

"Daddy makes sure we know the history of various lands. Especially Nuhana. How come we haven't heard this story before?" Niya asks.

"It has been forbidden for anyone to speak of Xaden or Xalen."

"I still don't understand, what does that have to do with our parents?"

"Your parents lived in Nuhana at that time. I have a feeling your father and mother are somehow connected to that night, and now they are being summoned back. I've known your parents for a very long time and they've never spoken of their lives in Nuhana. The only thing they ever expressed to me concerning that night was that if they got summoned and told me to take you two home, I had to get you there at all costs."

"That doesn't make sense. We left our home! Where are we going?"

"You'll see in time, my dear. Ah, we are here."

Niya and Keon look to see Port Ambit emerge as they continue over a hill. The ocean breeze flows over them, salty sea air filling their lungs. Wide grins spread over their faces as they study the hustle and bustle of the market vendors in various stages of closing their shops for the day. The aroma of fish and other sea life permeate the air as they make their way through the town.

"Look at those!" Keon blurts at the sight of the poorly constructed buildings.

"What?" Niya replies.

"The houses, they're stacked on top of each other."

"Big deal."

"And the roads are bouncy. Ahh-ahh-ahh." Keon's voice fluctuates with the vibration of the carriage.

"It's just the carriage wheels hitting the cobble-stone road," Niya snaps in annoyance.

"Ahh-ahh-ahh-ahh-ahhh."

"Stop it! You're so annoying."

"You're annoying."

"Your face is annoying."

"Enough!" Miss Lupita reprimands. "You two should be ashamed of your behavior. Now, the tavern is just up the road. I think all of us could use some time out of this carriage."

They continue down the road. Children in alleyways levitate and play with their gifts, filling Niya with envy.

A building taller than the rest stands out between the rundown buildings. A wooden sign hangs on the corner of the building, bright, white letters proclaiming it to be Joe's Tavern. Unlike the other buildings in town, the tavern had fresh dark-blue paint and white trim outlining the windows and door. A hag of a woman sat next to the door, panhandling for change.

Miss Lupita directs Fransisco and Francine to a nearby tie-post close to the front door. She exits the carriage and ties the fish-horses to the post. Niya and Keon quickly follow behind her as she heads toward the tavern. With a glance at the hag, Miss Lupita stops and looks the children deep in their eyes. "The people in this place will be friendly and kind to you, but do not trust anyone. Stay close to me and do exactly what I say."

They nod in agreement as Lupita turns back around, pulls a few coins out of her pocket and drops them into the hag's pan.

"Thank you, ma'am! Thank you," the hag says gratefully.

With a nod and a kind smile, Lupita leads the children into the tavern.

Inside, people are laughing and drinking, eating at tables made of barrels with thick wooden slabs placed on top. A piano collects dust in the far corner. In the back stands a bar, and Lupita strides towards it with the children following close behind her. A beautiful, dark-skinned woman with long purple locks flowing down her back stands behind the bar, cleaning a tall glass with a towel.

"It's been a long time, Joe," Lupita says with a smile.

Joe continues wiping the glass, not responding to Lupita's greeting.

"Josephine!" Lupita raises her voice, unsure whether Joe heard her. "Don't tell me you don't remember me? I sent you a sparrow saying I was coming. Didn't you get it?"

A blank expression remains on Joe's face as she continues cleaning the glass. Awkwardness fills the air, the silence becoming louder. All the patrons in the bar have their attention focused on Lupita and the children.

"Yes, I received the sparrow. Please have a seat. I'll pour you a drink," Joe says in a monotone voice. Her once-vibrant island accent is gone.

"This isn't like you," Lupita says, puzzled. "I don't under—" Lupita grabs the kids by their shoulders and slowly backs away from the bar. "Actually, we're good. We'll ease on out of here and be on our way."

When they turn around, everyone in the tavern is on their feet and closing in on them.

Lupita tightens her grip on the children's shoulders. "Okay, we won't ease out of here."

"What's wrong with them?" Keon asks.

"Head toward the door," Miss Lupita says before nudging them to move. They slowly walk past a few people before a man grabs Niya's arm.

"Get off me!" Niya yells and in the same monotone voice as Joe spoke, he says,

"We cannot allow you to leave."

Lupita turns, delivering a swift kick to the man's chest that sends him flying into the others behind him.

42

"Fight your way to the door!" she yells to the children as she takes a defensive stance.

"I've never had to fight before," Keon says as the crowd begins to grab at them.

Lupita holds off the emotionless bar patrons with a dance of timed punches and kicks. "There's a first time for everything. Get to the door!"

Keon and Niya head to the door, doing their best to fight through the crowd. Keon flips, kicks, and dodges people's advances, while Niya uses her telekinesis to fling bottles, plates, and people into those trying to grab them.

Just before the three of them reach the door, they notice the hag standing in the doorway. The hag's clothes and appearance morph into a clean, elite warrior in grayish-white armor that hugs her athletic physique. She takes out the coins Lupita dropped in her pan and lets them fall to the floor. As they fall, the coins shift into two metal clones of Lupita. The clones kneel on the ground.

"Get them," the warrior commands in a sinister voice. The clones lunge toward them. Miss Lupita grabs one clone by the arm, slinging it to the floor. Niya twists and extends her leg low, tripping the other clone just as Keon sidesteps and sends a swift kick to its head. Lupita follows her opponent's momentum to dodge each of its attack.

Using her gifts, Niya levitates the clone before flinging it toward Lupita. Seeing the air-bound clone, she quickly grabs the other clone. Using its own force against itself, she tosses it forward, and it slams into the incoming threat. The clones fall to the floor with a hard thud and crumble apart. Niya, Keon, and Miss Lupita stand together in a fighting position, looking at the former hag.

"Now that you're warmed up, let's begin," she says, reaching behind her back and pulling out a pair of katanas. Miss Lupita pushes Keon and Niya behind her as she steps forward. The warrior smirks and slams the hilts of her swords together, then twirls them toward Lupita.

"Get behind the bar!" Lupita commands the children as the warrior moves closer to her. In a swift movement, Lupita, grabs a barstool and tosses it at the former hag. With a simple raise of her arms, the warrior slashes the stool with a quick flick of her wrist. Sending splinters raining down on the ground as she continues advancing undeterred. Lupita rushes to grab another barstool, but the warrior's blade blocks her. Pain slices through Lupita's cheek and blood trickles down her face. The warrior lunges again, but Lupita pivots past the blade and lands an uppercut on the woman's chin. With an uneven step, she stumbles back, and Lupita quickly delivers a kick to the warrior's mid-section. The warrior drops her weapon as she grabs Lupita's leg, lifting Lupita and running, slamming her onto a nearby table. Bottles and glasses fly off the table and crash to the floor. Lupita stretches out her arm and grabs one of the falling glasses before it hits the ground, then smashes it against the former hag's head. The warrior's hands fly up to cradle her head, and she lets out a scream as Lupita gets to her feet. The warrior dives for her katanas, striking repeatedly at Lupita. Scraps of Lupita's clothes fly through the air and litter the floor as the warrior pins her into a corner. She points the tip of her blade at Lupita's throat, and Lupita winces at the sting of the blade piercing her skin. As blood trickles down her neck, a man in a blue and gray suit holding a black, silver-trimmed cane walks through the doorway.

Niya and Keon's faces light up before they run to him. They expel the word "Daddy!" as their lips open with gleeful relief.

"No!" Lupita yells. "It's Xaden!"

Keon and Niya freeze in their tracks, before stumbling back a few paces.

With a dark calmness in his voice, Xaden begins to speak. "Niece, Nephew, it's nice to finally meet you. Come, give your uncle a hug."

Unable to control their own movements, Keon and Niya inch over to Xaden and hug him.

"Good, stand here quietly, please. Don't move."

"Leave them alone!" Lupita shouts from the corner where the former hag has her cornered. "They have no part in this."

"They have every part in this. I need them. I even need you . . . Lupita, is it? Come here."

The warrior moves to the side, reluctantly sheathing the katana pointed at Lupita's throat. Lupita tries to resist Xaden's order, but her body moves against her will, only stopping once she reaches the kids.

Xaden flashes her a sinister smile. "I need you to stand here just as quietly as my niece and nephew while I speak with the lovely Qarinah." Xaden walks toward the hag-turned-warrior, shaking his head, his lips pulled back into a sneer. "Qarinah, Qarinah, Qarinah, Qarinah. I thought I told you not to engage with them?"

"They were going to leave before you arrived. I had to do something, my love."

"You are one of the few not affected by my gift. You're free will is why I care for you." He caresses the skin on her throat before tightening his fingers around it and pushing her back against the wall. "However, that is the same thing that drives me crazy . . . You do not touch them, is that clear?"

Qarinah swallows audibly. "Yes."

"Good." Xaden releases her before turning to face Lupita and the children. "You three, follow me. Do not make a sound and only do as I say. And that goes double for you, Niya. I can hear you rattling around in my head. Since you are so eager to assist, you can teleport all five of us to the location you see in my mind."

The five of them vanish into thin air, as Joe and the people in the tavern begin to awaken, dazed and confused.

Chapter 5: *A King's Request - Part 1*

In the throne room, Xolani looks down a long purple carpet at King Xerxes, sitting high on his golden throne in full royal garb. Ten council members sit on either side of the opulent throne, though their thrones are noticeably smaller. Four guards of different sizes and races stand on glowing circles behind the king. The glowing circles are similar to the ones outside the throne room. One glowing circle was empty.

That must be where Haygena stands. Xolani studies the guards' armor. Though their armor resembles Haygena's armor, there are slight differences—little marks signifying their home nations and tribes.

The walls of the throne are part of the Mother Tree, but something isn't right about them. Flashes of lightning courses across the walls and thunder rumbles faintly from the walls. Xolani walks forward until Haygena stops him. She kneels and motions for Xolani to do the same.

Reluctantly, Xolani sinks to one knee.

"My king," Haygena says after clearing her throat. "As requested, I have brought Xolani Raveness to you."

King Xerxes glares at them through narrowed hazel eyes. "You and the other members of the Five may go and stand at your posts outside the door," he says in a raspy, withered voice.

"Your Majesty?" Haygena questions.

"Leave us!" The command reverberates around the room.

"Yes, my king." Haygena glares at Xolani before rising to exit. The other members of the Five follow behind her, their footsteps synchronized.

"Council, you may leave as well."

Without hesitation, the council rises and begins to leave. A familiar face passes Xolani.

"Rashid?" Xolani whisper-yells as he reaches out and grabs him. Rashid turns to look at him. When they lock eyes, Xolani sees the other man's eyes roam across his face, as if searching his brain for a memory of

Xolani's face. Rashid's eyes widen and a joyful smile inches across his face.

"Good to see you, old friend," Xolani says. "Do you know where my mother and sister are?"

"I must go." A somber expression replaces the joy on Rashid's face. "My king doesn't repeat his commands."

"Wait, can't we—" But before he can finish his question, Rashid scurries out with the remaining council members. As the enormous doors close, the sound of the locks clicking into place echo through the empty room. Xolani stands at the base of the throne, meeting King Xerxes' intense stare. The years have not been kind to the king. His brown skin is wrinkled with the burdens of the throne, his hair whitened with time and stress. His once-regal body now withered and feeble.

Xolani straightens his spine and keeps his stance stiff. "Your Majesty, I am here. What do you request of my wife and me?"

King Xerxes glares at Xolani before rolling his shoulders back and puffing out his chest. "Let's not stand on ceremony, Xalen."

"King Xerxes, I have renounced that name. I am Xolani."

"Renounced?" King Xerxes laughs, the sound bitter and full of disdain. "Or changed it to hide your true identity, my son? I admit, it took a number of years to find you. You and that fugenie you keep as your wife."

"She is not powerless or weak!" Xolani snaps. "She may not be royalty or from an influential house, but she is my hidaya, my queen. And I will protect her with my life."

"How can you vow to protect anyone with a life that isn't yours? Your life was marked for death when you killed Xaden."

"Xaden caused his own death! I was merely protecting myself."

"It doesn't matter. You were sentenced for your actions, but instead of facing the consequences, you ran away to live a coward's life." King Xerxes' lips pull back in a snarl, his nose wrinkling in disgust.

"I am no coward!"

"Do not forget your place, boy!" King Xerxes' body mass inflates, making him larger. "You say you are no coward . . . prove it and your debt will be paid."

Xolani lifts an eyebrow and tilts his head slightly. "I owe no debt. My life is my own."

Rage contorts King Xerxes' face. "Your life belongs to me! The years have made you disrespectful and forgetful. You would do best to remember your place, Xalen."

Xolani rubs a hand over his temple as if warding off a headache. "No, the years have given me clarity. I don't enjoy having my time wasted."

"Jou stuk gemors!" King Xerxes yells in the royal dialect, his anger radiating off him as he sits up.

"Ek bedoel geen disrespek teenoor Pa nie," Xolani replies in a gentle tone before switching back to the common tongue. "I spoke from frustration. What does the king wish of me?"

King Xerxes leans back in his chair and strokes his white hair as he returns to his regular size. "The Creator may have given you more gifts than most," the king says in a condescending tone, "but I will still squash you like the nothing you are. You were never destined to be the Scion."

Xolani clenches his fists to keep his rage from boiling over.

"It is the Lumastar from the lightning forest that I desire," King Xerxes says.

"The Lumastar." Xolani chuckles. "The mythical star created by the man of light, which, if legend is right, is being held captive by a kwane?"

"The lightning bird, yes."

"I think you are too old to believe in fairy tales."

Xolani's words are drowned out by the king pounding his fists on the throne's armrests. "It's no fairytale! It's real."

Xolani laughs, shaking his head in disbelief. "I cannot believe you brought me all this way . . . for a fairytale."

48

"It's no"—King Xerxes coughs hard—"fairytale." After wiping his mouth with the back of his hand, the king continues, "It is as real as you and I."

"You have an army with some of the best warriors from every country, why do you need me? And why now?"

"I wanted my son."

"You expect me to believe that sentiment?"

"It's the truth," King Xerxes says.

"Where was that truth when you called for my execution?!"

"You killed your brother! The law is the law, what would you have had me do?"

"Xaden's death was not my fault. You know that," Xolani says with an angry passion. "You tried to have me executed to save your Legacy. You didn't want a blemish, the black mark you called your son, to be in your precious royal house, and if Xaden couldn't rule, then—"

"I will not tolerate such blatant disrespect!" King Xerxes struggles to his feet, only to fall back onto his throne. Winded, he says, "Your brother's death was a tragedy and the kingdom mourned him. No one cared about you when they thought you dead, Xalen."

"You were waiting for an opportunity to get rid of me from the day Xaden and I were born! Say what you will, Xaden was an egotistical maniac who took pleasure in making others do his bidding against their will. The kingdom feared him and what his rule would've looked like, whether you want to admit that or not."

"You were always dramatic and jealous of your brother's greatness," King Xerxes says. "I'm glad the kingdom has no memory of you." The last words barely come out as King Xerxes grabs his chest and cringes with pain.

"Father!" Xolani rushes forward, concern making him forget about his animosity towards the man. "What's wrong?"

The king swats Xolani's hand away. "Xalen, I don't have a lot of time left. I have a type of neuralgia decay that will kill me. I need you to retrieve the Lumastar. Please."

Xolani thinks for a minute before kneeling and looking his father in the eye. "You could have sent any or all of the Five to retrieve the Lumastar. Why is it so important to get it now, and why me?"

King Xerxes leans back in his throne before placing his hands on the armrest. "You are the one I can trust. I'm sure there are whispers about my health, but, apart from the royal physician, no one knows I am dying."

"That may be true, but why now?" Xolani asks in a skeptical tone.

King Xerxes closes his eyes for a moment. "The Mother Tree is dying. My scholars and I are not sure how, but our best guess is that someone poisoned her with a lightning virus."

"Then you've communed with the Mother Tree and that's what made you sick?"

King Xerxes nods in agreement. "Now you understand. In the morning, you, Haygena, and a few of my guards will go—"

"No. We will leave before nightfall."

The old man leans forward. "Why?"

"If the stories are true, the kwane is similar to other birds and less likely to be active at night. If we leave now, we can arrive by nightfall and be out before first light."

"Very well. I will have a combat fighter prepped while Haygena takes you to the armory. She and the remaining Five will accompany you to retrieve the Lumastar."

"She can take me to the armory, but I'm not taking her or any of your soldiers with me. I need a small crew. Raine, Rashid, and Gibbon will be fine."

"This mission is too important for your lackeys. You will take my warriors."

"No! I will take those I know and trust."

King Xerxes strokes a strand of his hair. "You still don't trust me?" He sighs. "Very well, go tonight and take whomever you wish, but if you come back without the Lumastar, Keon, Niya and . . . wait, what was your fugenie's—oh, that's right, Raine. They will all pay the price."

Xolani clenches his jaw as he and his father lock eyes. Neither man moves. Heat rages through Xolani as the threat to his family echoes in his mind. Fists clenched, the blood pulsing in his hand warns him to calm down.

"I will do this for you, Father," he says. "But after this, my family lives without your shadow looming over us, agreed?"

"I care less of you or your family. Bring me the Lumastar."

Xolani turns and heads for the enormous locked doors. Thoughts of his family bolts across his mind and he turns again to face his father.

"I need to see Mother and Ada before I go."

"You have no right to make demands."

"Either I see Mother and Ada, or you can find another for your quest."

"We don't have time for these childish games. The Mother Tree is dying as we speak. If it dies, our world will follow. You can see them once you've returned!"

"I have your word that I will be able to see Mother and Ada upon my return?"

"Yes, now go!" King Xerxes commands.

Xolani fights the urge to keep pushing. Instead, he turns and exits the throne room.

Once the throne room doors shut, a panel behind King Xerxes slides up, and Xaden emerges from the darkness.

Chapter 6: *A King's Request - Part 2*

Xaden struts forward, his chest puffed out as he makes his way to the front of his father's throne. His cane taps against the purple marble floor while he walks. He stops at the foot of the throne and takes a knee as he bows his head.

"Did you locate Xalen's half-breed children?" King Xerxes asks, his voice booming through the throne room.

"Yes, Father. I found them just outside the Aberrant Territory in Port Ambit. What are your orders?"

"Take them to the detention cells," the king commands. "I will have two of the Five sent down to guard them. After that, I want you to go to the Lightning Forest, retrieve the Lumastar from Xalen, and ensure he is returned alive."

"Alive? I want him dead!" Xaden lifts his head, fire burning in his wide-stretched eyes. "His time is up and mine will be shortly! Why didn't you send an extraction team to retrieve him instead of that buffoon Gibbon?"

"You dare question me!" King Xerxes roars. "The one who's kept you alive all these years? If it wasn't for me, your consciousness would still be floating around in an empty void. Qarinah would still be begging for scraps while trying to piece your mind together with that corpse of a body you have now!"

"I'm not questioning you, my king," Xaden says. "I merely spoke out of frustration and confusion. I thought—"

"That's the problem—you thought." King Xerxes adjusts himself to sit tall in his throne. "I will not go over this with you again. Qarinah took too long to bring me your corpse after your mind separated from it. We did all we could to keep your body from decomposing, but a living host is what we need to make the transference complete. Xalen, is the perfect genetic living host because he is your twin. You need his body and I need the Lumastar. An extraction team could've ended badly. I needed someone non-threatening to fetch him."

"I don't care. He deserves to die for what he did."

King Xerxes rubs the bridge of his nose. "It should be an easy task for him to retrieve the star and return with it. And then, once you've taken over his body, he will cease to exist, isn't that enough? But if it's not, in the event that we need to expedite his demise, we have three other viable candidates to transfer your consciousness to."

"Fine," Xaden mumbles. "I will go and retrieve the Lumastar and Xalen, but I need to take the children with me."

King Xerxes strokes another lock of white hair. "Why?"

Xaden's lips curl into a malicious grin. "Xalen will be willing to do anything to save them. It will unbalance him."

As Xaden rises to his feet, King Xerxes says, "Xaden, do I have your loyalty?" He glares at Xaden from the corner of his eye.

"Of course, Father," Xaden says. He leaps forward to grab King Xerxes' hand, kisses it, then gently places his father's hand back on the armrest of the throne.

"Good, just make sure you bring back the Lumastar."

"Yes, my king." Xaden gives a deep bow, then strides back to the open panel behind the throne. Qarinah is leaning against the panel frame, an evil smile playing on her lips. She slides a katana out from behind her back, miming a kill stroke in King Xerxes' direction. Xaden smiles, waving a hand against her proposal. She shrugs and turns to exit as Xaden follows through the closing panel.

Chapter 7: *The Scion Quest*

The sun paints the fading blue sky with hues of pink, orange, and red as Xolani, Raine, Rashid, and Gibbon fly high above the clouds in a CF-4 prototype. The sky above them is clear and clouds flow like an ember sea beneath them. Gibbon and Raine are seated in the cockpit, relaxing in their seats as the large jet cruises on auto-pilot. Laughter bellows from the rear of the jet, and Rashid's deep voice radiates through the interior as he jokes with Xolani,

"It's bad luck to have a plane with no name."

"Superstitious?" Xolani teases.

"Of course not, but we really should give this new bird a name. How about Lucy?" Rashid suggests.

Xolani's eyes close and lips tighten as he shakes his head in disapproval.

"Okay, I got it . . . Bella."

Xolani lifts his brow and shakes his head again.

"No?" Rashid frowns slightly, then looks past Xolani into the cockpit. "What do you two think?"

Raine and Gibbon glance at one another before Raine says, "Keep trying. And why does the plane have to be named after a woman? How do you know the plane isn't a guy? Is there some dangling part that I didn't see when we boarded?"

A thick blanket of silence falls over the jet as Rashid pretends to be intrigued with his seat.

Gibbon clears his throat before speaking softly. "How about Adventurer?"

"What's that?" Xolani asks.

"Adventurer, for the plane, I mean the name of the plane. Adventurer?"

Gibbon's cheeks turn scarlet as they all turn to look at him. He gives a nervous grin.

"Actually," Rashid says as he nods, "that's actually, not half bad . . . Adventurer."

Xolani and Raine motion in agreement as Gibbon's teeth shine through his emerging smile.

The plane becomes quiet again until Rashid says, "So, a country man, and in the Aberrant territory no less? That must have been tough. I never would have guessed the suave model I used to know would become a simple country farmer."

"We don't farm, it's just a small garden," Xolani says.

"Same difference, man! I'm just saying, you're the same guy who spent hours to get ready for an event, only to still make us late. The same guy who needed to coordinate his outfits the week prior to the event."

Xolani chuckles. "That only happened once."

"Once!" Rashid bursts out. "What about Kumbak's coronation?"

"That has nothing to do with me getting ready or coordinating out-fits." Xolani laughs. "You just wanted a reason to bring that up."

"Bring what up?" Raine calls from the cockpit,

"Nothing," Xolani blurts, giving Rashid a disapproving look. "Rashid is talking about nothing."

"Nothing?" Rashid ignores Xolani's look. "Punching the Amerigo's head of state is not nothing."

"First of all," Xolani says as he puts a finger into the air, "Kumbak was not head of state at the time that I punched him. Second of all, he de-served it."

"Yeah, he did," Rashid jokes. The two men laugh good-naturedly for a moment. "But, man, we got into some trouble when we got back to the palace."

"My mother yelled at me for a week," Xolani says, his smile slowly fading as he remembers his mother and sister. "How are my Mother and Ada doing since my death?"

Rashid lowers his head, but not before Xolani sees the joy draining from his face. He fidgets in his seat, twisting his hands together. After a moment, he breathes in deeply. "The king had your execution broadcasted on every feed."

"Wait, what execution?" Xolani says with equal surprise and disguise. "Why? Did someone die in my place? Who was it?"

Rashid shrugs. "I honestly don't know. The person's head was covered. I guess, he still needed to make an example for Xaden's death."

Xolani lowers his gaze to the floor and turns away from Rashid. "I didn't think someone would die in my place."

"Look, I'm sorry man," Rashid says as he leans in. "I know you didn't mean for another person to die, but we all make decisions that ripple into other's lives, whether we want them to or not." He reaches out and claps Xolani on the shoulder. "During your match against Xaden, the people waited to hear that you would be triumphant, but not at the loss of his life. We all knew the law for killing . . . But I couldn't stand by and let you be executed for defending yourself from an enraged psychopath. I had to help you escape, so that guy's death is on my head as much as it is yours. Seeing you after all these years is a blessing from the Creator, and we should never forget that. I do, however, slightly fear the compounded repercussions of my actions once the king finds out I helped you escape."

"He will not find out from me, my friend." Xolani turns back around. "Rashid, my mother and sister, how are they?"

"Right, well, Ada . . . you've already seen her." Rashid rubs his chin.

Xolani's forehead wrinkles into a frown. "I haven't seen her."

"You have. Haygena, she's Ada or is it that Ada is Haygena? I don't know. Either way, she's Haygena now."

"That cold-hearted warrior of a woman is—was—my little sister? My sweet, innocent, little. sister?"

"Yes."

"How? Why?"

"I'm not sure. King Xerxes sent her away shortly after you were, um, executed. She returned some years later as Haygena, and was made to be one the Five. She quickly became the leader. To be honest, I'm not sure she even knows who she is at this point."

They sit in silence as Xolani pushes through the disbelief. Did he even want to know about his mother?

"And my mother?"

"I'm sorry, Xalen—I mean Xolani," Rashid stutters.

"Lani is fine."

"Why didn't you keep your actual name? Did you really think the king wouldn't find you?"

"Honestly, I didn't think he'd waste his time. He never liked me growing up—you remember what it was like for me there. He was just waiting for a reason to get rid of me. I spent my childhood trying to please him, just for him to give his attention and undying love to Xaden."

"I remember, but look at you now. I'm proud of you." Rashid smiles.

"Thank you. I'm not sure how we got to speaking of my childhood, but please tell me about my mother. Did she disappear or something?"

"No. Perhaps. No one has seen Lady Neyma for many years." Rashid leans back in his chair and lets out a heavy sigh. "After you and Xaden were gone, she was understandably devastated. And I'm sure it didn't help when your father brought his mistresses to live in the castle. I believe that once your sister left, she really went over the edge. King Xerxes had a small cottage built on the inside of the earth ring. No one is allowed in that area of the palace grounds, at all. As far as I know, that's where Lady Neyma is."

Xolani stares at nothing as he ponders over that information. "Well, at least they're alive. I'm thankful for that."

"I wish I could give you better news, but things have not gone well since you've been gone, Lani. Power outages on the outer rim of the city, resistance fighters building support against the throne, and, oh, do you remember Qarinah?"

"Vaguely. She and Xaden were together or something, right?"

Rashid nods. "Since his death, she's spent her family's fortune trying to find ways to bring Xaden back. Now that she's broke, she panhandles from town to town. Sad, but I would be lying if I said I didn't find some enjoyment in her current situation."

"That is unfortunate. Qarinah and Xaden were two peas in a very cruel pod, but I wouldn't want—"

"Sir," Gibbon says, turning his head slightly. "We're coming in range of the lightning forest."

"So stop gossiping," Raine says.

Xolani ignores his wife's comment. "Take us off auto-pilot and find somewhere to land. Stay about a quarter of a mile out from the lightning forest. We don't want to pose a threat."

"Sir," Gibbon interjects, "the auto-pilot would be more efficient at locating and guiding us down to a desired spot. In fact, the Adventurer's on-board computer is so advanced, I'm sure it could fight an army with very little assistance from us. I mean, its new Mach-15 core system is the most advanced system to date—"

"Hopefully," Xolani interrupts with a smile, "it won't come to us relying on a computer to fight for us. I'm sure you're quite capable of landing safely."

Gibbon returns the smile with a nod.

The group peers out of the front of the plane. In the distance, a huge tower of light stretches from the ground into the heavens, the beam brightening as the last glimmer of sunlight fades into the night. Gibbon pulls back on the throttle, slowing their approach.

Raine uses the controls on the console to assist with the descent through the clouds. The surprisingly bright landscape's vast view decreases as they descend. Raine points to an open spot, and Gibbon gently guides the plane down for a soft landing. They hear the hissing of the airlines as the weight of the plane buckles a little under the pressure of the landing gear touching the ground. Behind Xolani and Rashid, a quick pop and a gush of air breaks the seal of the cabin's pressure as the back wall slowly lowers itself to the ground. They unfasten their seatbelts and head to the cargo area to gear up.

Xolani notices Gibbon placing equipment in a pile and says, "Gibbon, we need you to stay here with the plane."

"Sir?"

"In the event that things don't go as planned, we need you ready to take off and fly us out of here quickly."

Gibbon nods at the command and returns the gear to its original spot.

Xolani rests his hand on Gibbon's shoulder. "Put on the gear. Everyone has a role to fill. Through her studies, Raine knows the kwane mythology. Rashid is a brilliant strategist when he's focused, and you, you are an outstanding pilot, who, when push comes to shove, might just be the reason we survive."

A smile grows on Gibbons face as he grabs his gear and moves into the cockpit. Xolani watches him for a second before turning to suit up. He looks over to the bottom of the ramp where Rashid is standing in his dark boots and black cargo pants, a baton strapped to each leg. His fitted gray shirt shows off his muscular physique as a sleek military bag rests on his back and a pair of goggles hangs around his neck. Rashid smiles as he converses with Raine, who is dressed in a similar fashion. Instead of batons, Raine has a short, metal bō staff strapped to her back and is wearing a black, short-sleeved, button-up shirt. Goggles also rest around her neck.

Xolani refocuses on getting ready and looks down at his gear. Grabbing a protective vest, he feels the heaviness of it as he lifts it from the bench. He raises it over his head and lets the weight of the vest slide down his arms. It comes to a blunt stop as the weight drops onto his shoulders and slams into his chest. Memories flood his mind as the familiar feel of the heavy vest reminds him of strict royal training and pointless recon missions. He quickly pushes past the memories and continues suiting up. He fastens a pair of dark-metal gauntlets around his forearms. Finally, he picks up a pair of single-lens goggles, and pulls them down past his head to let them rest around his neck before making his way down the ramp.

At the end of the ramp, he turns back to Gibbon. "If we're not back by daybreak, leave."

He takes Raine's hand. "We both don't need to go. You should stay with Gibbon."

"Lani," Raine says with a stern smile. "I'm going."

"If things go sideways, at least the kids will still have you."

Raine steps closer. "Don't talk like that. Everything will be fine. Let's get in, get out, so we can be back home in time for breakfast."

Xolani places his hand on her cheek gently and they exchange smiles.

With a playful smile, Raine says, "Besides, I'm a better fighter."

"Are you now?"

Raine nods and leans in to kiss her husband.

"Geez," Rashid mutters. "We haven't even started yet and you two are already all over each other! I feel like we're teenagers again. Can we go before the two of you need a room?"

Raine and Xolani roll their eyes before heading out to begin their quest into the lightning forest. The grass thins as they draw nearer to the tree line, dust drifting up as their boots connect with the dry dirt on the barren ground.

"Raine, any idea where we can find the kwane or the man of light?" Rashid asks from the tail end of the group.

"The kwane should be nesting somewhere in the middle of the lightning forest. The man of light will most likely be in the kwane's nest. When we descended, I noticed a small mountain south of our current location. I'm sure the kwane will have a cave or large burrow in the mountain as its nest."

Rashid sighs heavily. "I see . . . so, there's not much planning we can do. Just find the cave or burrow, hope the kwane is asleep, then find the man of light with the Lumastar?"

"Yep, simple," Raine says as she pulls and settles her goggles on her eyes. Rashid and Xolani follow her example.

"Sure, simple," Rashid says sarcastically as he shakes his head. "You know, it's hard to make up a good strategy if I don't have the proper intel." Rashid stops walking and flings his arms wide, moving them through the air. "Simple things. Like, how big is it, eating habits, even a mating ritual would be something."

"What is your problem?" Xolani says with a pinched face, as he and Raine turn to look at Rashid.

Rashid backs up a step. "How hard can that be?"

"Stop!" Raine yells. "You're about to back into a lightning tree!"

Rashid, who hadn't realized they'd walked into the forest, now sees the thousands of lightning trees surrounding them. Carefully, he inches forward, turning to get a better look. "It's like the lightning is encased in glass as it shoots up from the ground," he says in amazement.

Xolani and Raine move closer, and Raine examines the tree with Rashid.

"It's splendid, but we must keep going. We're losing moonlight, and we'll need every moment of it," Xolani says, placing a hand on Rashid's shoulder to steer him away from the trees.

"Right," Rashid replies, and the trio trudge forward again, their goggles protecting them from the bright flashes of lightning inside each passing tree.

"It looks as if we're about to reach the base of the mountain. How do we find the kwane's nest? Can you feel its location, Raine?"

"My gifts only allow me to sense those I know, Rashid. The better I know them, the better I can feel their presence. My goggles, on the other hand, can track bio-signatures."

"What?" Rashid asks, his tone filled with uncertainty.

"My goggles are . . . every living thing has some type of marker within them that is readable, you just need the right equipment. I normally use these goggles to assist me in my research, but since this forest is all but a barren wasteland, I figured the goggles would make it easy to track since they're the only creatures in here. We have been tracking what seems to be a man. He should be just ahead, in a small cave at the bottom of the mountain."

"That's odd," Rashid says, concerned. "Don't you think?"

"What's odd?" Raine asks.

"That the man is in a cave at the bottom of the mountain."

"I'm not following," Raine says.

Rashid stops walking, causing her and Xolani to do the same. "The man is supposed to be a captive of the kwane, right?"

"What's your point?" Raine says.

Rashid sighs. "A mythical *bird* made of *lightning*, nesting in *a cave* at the *bottom* of the *mountain* . . . I thought birds nested in trees or way up high on mountain tops. This just seems iffy to me, like we're walking into a trap."

"How deep in the cave is he?" Xolani asks.

"Not far," Raine answers. "About nine meters past the entrance. I think Rashid is right. I didn't notice it before, but he's just standing still."

"Why, that's not unusual at all," Rashid remarks.

"We've been following his bio signature for about forty minutes. For twenty minutes of that time, I've been able to see his outline. It hasn't moved at all. I didn't notice it until now, but I agree, Rashid. This might be a trap."

They stand around, pondering their next move.

"Are you able to see any other entrances or exits where the man is standing?" Rashid asks.

Raine turns and touches the temple of her goggles with two fingers. "It doesn't appear so . . . but I can't be completely sure. These goggles weren't designed for topography. I can only see partial densities in the mountain."

"That should be good enough. I have a plan," Rashid says with a playful grin.

Chapter 8: *A Grand Entrance*

The hairs on the back of Xolani's neck stand on end as a chill runs down his spine and he enters the dark cave. The loud silence dissipates as the dirt shifts beneath his boots when he inches forward. Raising his arm to chest level, Xolani snaps his finger. A bright flame engulfs his extended finger. With the flicker of the new light, a dark silhouette of a man takes form as Xolani's eyes adjust in the dim light. He moves forward.

"Sir," he says softly, but the man doesn't acknowledge him. He clears his throat and raises his voice. "Sir, are you the man of light?" When he still gets no reply, Xolani inches closer. "Are you the man being held by the kwane? Do you know where I can find the Lumastar?"

"No man unworthy may be given the Lumastar," the man says in a monotone voice.

Xolani steps closer. "It's vital that I talk to you about the Lumastar. It's important I retrieve it."

"Be careful, Xolani," the man answers in a familiar and sinister voice. "Your time is up."

Xolani reaches out to turn the man by the shoulder but quickly pulls his hand back. Heat radiates from the man as he twists and contorts towards Xolani.

"No one can have the Lumastar, no one!"

Transparent white feathers begin to sprout all over the man. Black, razor-sharp claws protrude and elongate from his hands and feet. Xolani tries to retreat, but his feet are rooted to the ground. He's lost the ability to blink as he stands in full view of the horrific transformation.

The man is the kwane!

A jagged beak becomes visible and the man's face is now indistinguishable from that of a bird in the flickering light. Short bursts of lightning shoot out and jump from feather to feather as the monster stretches to its full frightening form. Xolani tries to back up, but the kwane locks its fiery red eyes on him and lets out a thunderous squall. Xolani throws his hands up to cover his ears in defense. It flaps its wings, hovering briefly before slamming its wings together and sending forth a booming wave of sound, vaulting Xolani through the air and out of the cave. Xolani crashes into the ground and tumbles through the dirt. With a few flaps of its wings, the kwane glides out of the cave and soars up into the night sky, the moonlight shining through its massively stretched wings highlighting the horrific beauty of the beast. High in the sky, the kwane begins to circle as it aims to locate its prey.

Disoriented, Xolani hears a diminishing ringing in his ear. The distorted sound of Raine and Rashid running toward him becomes clearer as they yell for him to get up. He stumbles to his feet as they pull him up by his arms. Rashid and Raine carry him, while trying to sprint to the tree line.

"That was not the plan," Rashid says before the kwane swoops down and latches its talons into his shoulders. He lets out a primal scream as the talons dig deeper into him. As volts of electricity course through him, the agony in his voice pierces the others' ears. The kwane flaps its wings, lifting him off the ground. Rashid struggles against the kwane's grip. He swings to punch at the massive bird as Xolani and Raine tug at his legs. Their boots dig into the dirt as they hold on to Rashid until a surge of electricity flings Raine and Xolani backwards. Rashid's yells trail off as the kwane carries him into the night sky. Xolani and Raine call out to Rashid, but their voices fade into the black of the night. They look into the distance, hoping for a glimpse of their friend, but to no avail.

Silence creeps in with the growing crisp night air. A familiar twinge pulls at Raine's stomach. She turns and a rush of adrenaline tingles through her body as she grabs Xolani's arm. He breaks her hold to speak, but as he turns around, whatever he was about to say disappears from his mind.

Xaden, Niya, Keon, Lupita, and Qarinah emerge from the shadows of the dark cave, all wearing goggles to protect their eyes. The night lights up with emotions as the shock of seeing their family with Xaden cuts deep into their souls. The cold and empty expressions on their children's faces cause a void to hit the pit of Xolani and Raine's core. Raine moves toward them but Xolani grabs her hand to stop her.

"Come to me," Xaden shouts, holding his cane loosely in front of him. Flashes of lightning fill the sky and a terrifying shriek is heard from above. The kwane speeds toward Xaden and comes to a stop a few feet from the ground as it glides to drop beside him.

"You're alive? How can this be?" Xolani asks. His question is met with a cold, hard stare from Xaden and those surrounding him. What seems like an eternity passes in silence before Xaden takes a few steps forward.

"I told you, your time is up, brother." He raises his cane, pointing it in Xolani and Raine's direction. In a harsh whisper, he says, "Get them."

Niya and Keon rush forward to attack their parents as the kwane screeches, extending its talons before following the children. Lupita waves her hands in circular motions, shifting the dirt and swirling it up toward her hands. Two humanoid rock creatures take shape, and with a flick of her wrist, the rock creatures sprint forward to join the fight. Xolani and Raine split up, Raine moving to intercept the kids while Xolani fights the kwane and Lupita's rock creatures.

Xaden and Qarinah stand back and wait in amusement as they observe their orchestrated chaos. Xolani avoids making contact with the kwane as he defends himself against the rock creatures.

"How do we break Xaden's hold over them?" Raine yells, dodging and deflecting their children's violent advances with her bō staff.

Xolani extends his open hand toward the rock creatures. "Cognitive recalibration!" With one swift motion, he closes his fist, pulling his arms back into his body. A boulder-sized piece of earth erupts from beneath the rock creatures.

"What do you mean?" Raine replies.

Xolani flicks his wrist, flinging the boulder high above the rock creatures and dropping it down. "We need to reboot their brains."

"Reboot their brains?"

"Hit them on the head!" Xolani yells, wiping the sweat from his brow.

"I'm not hitting our children on their heads."

"Raine, I'm a little busy," Xolani says as the kwane rushes through the air. He catches the attack from the corner of his eye and flips over the descending kwane. Bringing both hands together, he releases a powerful burst of wind, and the kwane crashes through the dirt. The creature grinds to a halt, quickly repositioning itself for another attack. It launches at Xolani, who stands with his chest out and chin high. He makes circular motions with his arms, gathering moisture from the air and shooting a massive blast of water at the kwane. Its eyes widen, beak falling open as an agonizing scream tumbles out. As the electricity flowing around its body slowly fizzles out, the creature stumbles. The kwane presses its elbows to its side, clutching itself before reverting back into a man and dropping to the ground.

Xolani's head suddenly jerks as Lupita spears him in the back. She wraps her arms around his waist as his hands fly into the air and tackles him to the ground, unleashing a barrage of punches to his spine and kidneys.

Raine, not wanting to hurt her children, continues to deflect and re-direct their advancing attacks. She moves to swing her bō staff, but an invisible force holds her in place. Unable to control her body, her arms fling into the air as her legs spread apart. Keon twists, landing two swift kicks—first with his left, then with his right—to his mother's midsection, sending her flying back into the dirt. Niya uses her gifts to keep her mother pinned to the ground as Keon lands on top of Raine and proceeds to send punch after punch into her body.

Lupita delivers a fury of attacks on Xolani's back. Placing his palms on the ground, Xolani launches himself up with a quick burst, throwing her off his back. He grabs Lupita's arm and sends her catapulting through the air.

Keon is caught off guard in his attack as Lupita hurtles towards him and knocks him off his mother. Lupita and Keon fly past Niya, causing her to break her hold on Raine as they land on a lightning tree. The pair screams as their bodies flail from the electricity coursing through them. Raine, now free, quickly grabs her bō staff and absorbs the grip's rubber properties. She runs to the tree, dropping the bō staff and sending a kick to their bodies. Shakily, she watches the pair fall lifelessly to the ground.

Xolani rushes to Raine's side and doesn't hear Xaden shout to Niya, "Bring them to me."

As he bends to comfort Keon, Xolani's body is frozen and finds himself unable to move. Raine tries to move, but finds herself in the same predicament as Xolani. Their bodies hover in the air as Niya turns them around and floats them over to Xaden. With a devilish grin, Xaden looks Xolani in the eyes and says,

"My brother, my dear foolish brother. How have you been?"

"I've had better days, Xaden," Xolani says wryly.

"I'm sure you have. You actually married the fugenie Lareina."

"The last time we spoke, I told you never to call her that slur again," Xolani snaps.

Xaden closes the gap between them with a few steps. "Yes," Xaden says as their noses almost touch. "I remember. Then you tried to kill me."

Xolani stares Xaden down. "I was defending myself. I did what I had to do."

"Retaliation," Xaden replies with a smile. "Xalen, an eye for an eye leaves us both blind." He pulls his collar to the side, revealing a mesh of dark, burnt skin that pulls and twists against the rest of his skin. "That's very bad form, old boy, very bad form." With a wicked smile, Xaden punches Xolani in the stomach.

Gasping for breath, Xolani says, "Am I supposed to feel sorry for you? We all have scars. You were my brother."

"Yes, I was your brother. Now, not so much, I guess. Luckily, I have instincts, too. My mind was astro-projected into another plane. If not for my dear Qarinah, I might still be floating around aimlessly. But now I have a target, and I'm taking aim. Your time is up, Xolani, your time is up!"

"Just kill me and cut the theatrics," Xolani snaps. "You've always been overly dramatic. Even when we were kids, you loved making every problem into a circus-level event."

"Oh, Xalen, let's not dwell on the past, shall we? I'm not here for that. It's on to bigger and better things for me. I'm here for the Lumastar." Smirking, he turned to Xolani's daughter. "Niya, be a dear. Release your parents and come stand over here."

Raine and Xolani drop to the ground with a hard thud as Niya takes her place next to Qarinah.

"Now . . . Qarinah, did you bring the dampening cuffs for our feathery lightning friend over here?"

Qarinah flips her hair back as she approaches Xaden, her hips swaying with every step. She assumes a pose that draws attention to her best attributes as she takes the dampening cuffs from a belt loop at her lower back.

"Of course, I have." She extends the cuffs to Xaden.

Xaden clenches his teeth as he glares at her. "Put them on it!"

Qarinah scurries to the kwane, grabbing its arms and pinning them to its back as she tightens the dampening cuffs around its wrists. She gives a nod to Xaden, who motions to Niya to levitate the kwane closer to them. Niya places the creature in front of Xaden, making it hunch over.

Pleased, Xaden returns his gaze to Xolani and Raine. "Now, for you two. I need you to ask this thing for the Lumastar."

"You ask," Xolani spits out.

"Let's not do the thing where you resist, then I threaten you, then you still resist, and then I kill someone you care about. Let's just go right into you doing what I say or, the next thing that will happen is that I will kill your unconscious half-breed fugenie son over there."

"How am I supposed to talk to it?" Xolani asks. His hands throb and he unclenches them. "It's not awake."

"Niya," Xaden says, his fierce gaze shooting through Xolani. "Use your telepathy to wake it up."

Niya closes her eyes and places two fingers on her temples. A moment passes before the kwane gasps and struggles to break free. The kwane shifts its emerald eyes back and forth, observing its surroundings.

"What's the meaning of this?" the kwane commands in a dual voice.

Xolani steps forward, bowing his head and kneeling. "Kwane—"

"I am not the kwane. I am Malkum."

"Malkum," Xolani says apologetically. "We are in need of your help."

"You control the kwane and then restrain me. You say one thing, but your actions say another."

"I understand how this must look, but it is crucial that we put that aside for the moment. The Mother Tree is dying. We believe the Lumastar can revive it. Do you have it?"

"There is always something," Malkum says with great exaggeration as he sighs heavily, "dying, dead or about to die with you mortals. I am so sick of it. But I will tell you how to get the Lumastar. You simply ask for it."

Xolani cocks his head to the side. "Ask for it?"

"Yes, the Lumastar comes to those who are worthy and need it most."

Not expecting it to be so easy, the group around Malkum look at one another.

"Ask already, you idiot!" Qarinah cries out in a shrill voice.

Xolani slants his eyes in her direction before re-engaging with Malkum. "Malkum, may I have the Lumastar?"

Malkum rolls his eyes. A moment passes, then his eyes roll back to reveal the whites as lightning flows through and around him. The lightning joins to flow through his chest and out his back in a circular pattern. Light emits from his chest, catching the lightning. Xolani shields his eyes as the light turns blinding. The light floats from Malkum's body, crystalizing into a pointy, polynomial star. The lightning that bounces furiously inside of it lessens as it continues to float into Xolani's outstretched hands.

The group stares in amazement at the Lumastar, until *BANG*! Xolani stands in shock as Malkum falls to his knees, his face smacking into the dirt. Xolani takes his eyes off Malkum to see a still-smoking gun in Xaden's hand pointed straight at him.

"This has been literally an illuminating experience, but I'm going to need that," Xaden says with an evil smirk.

Xolani glances at Raine. Her concerned emerald eyes tell Xolani to give Xaden the Lumastar.

Xolani extends his hand. "Take it!"

"I thought you'd see it my way." He snaps his fingers at Niya. "Niya, grab that for me, would you, dear?"

Niya looks at the Lumastar, and it begins to float over into Xaden's outstretched hand.

Admiring his stolen achievement, Xaden says, "And now, dear, dear brother, I must say goodbye." He points the gun at Xolani again.

Xolani closes his eyes, his heart pounding as he waits for Xaden to pull the trigger. Silence blankets the forest before the loud sound of the bullet exploding from the barrel echoes through the air.

Chapter 9: *At All Cost*

Xolani steps back but catches himself.

"What the—" Xaden yells as Xolani opens his eyes. The gun is pointed down and Xaden is nursing a wound in his hand. Everyone, including Xaden, is looking toward the tree line. Xolani follows their eyes just as a baton whizzes in that direction. Rashid rockets through the forest, catching the baton as he sprints to aid his companions. Qarinah rushes forward to stop him.

As Xaden watches Qarinah, Raine springs into action and kicks the gun out of Xaden's hand. Following her lead, Xolani steps forward, drawing his arm back and with his full might he lands a hard, right hook to Xaden's jaw. He continues his assault with an upper-cut to Xaden's stomach. Xolani is quick to land blow after blow on his brother's body. Xaden loses his grip on the Lumastar and it falls in the dirt. The brothers flow in a violent dance of punches and kicks against one another. Seizing the moment, Raine runs to Niya and grabs her by the shoulders.

"Niya! Snap out of it. You're stronger than this. Don't let Xaden control you! Break free!"

Niya doesn't respond, she simply stands there with a blank, lifeless expression on her face. Unwilling to give up, Raine grabs Niya's hand and pulls her toward Keon. But Niya doesn't move. Raine frowns, tension building in her stomach. She hugs Niya and kisses her on the forehead. Raine moves swiftly as the sounds of weapons clashing, punches connecting to body parts and battle grunts echo through the forest. She hurries to Keon and Lupita, whom are still lying on the dirt, barely breathing. Raine kneels between them.

"Can you both move?" she asks in a gentle but rushed tone. "We need to go."

"My arm," Lupita says with great strain on her face. "I can't feel it, but I think I can stand."

"Mommy, my body hurts," Keon cries.

"I know you're hurting, sweetie," Raine says. "But I need you to try to move. Let me help." She places Keon's arm around her shoulder and they rise. Though his legs are wobbly and unsteady, he manages to stand. He props his weight against Raine's as Lupita grasps her injured arm and slowly gets to her feet. Carefully, Raine shifts Keon's weight off her and onto Lupita. "There's a jet at the edge of the forest north of here. I need you to take him there. Gibbon, a friend, is piloting the plane. If we haven't returned by sunrise, leave us."

"We won't leave," Lupita says.

"You must," Raine says. She closes her eyes and lowers her head slightly before looking back up at the older woman. "The best thing to do now is to get you and Keon as far from here as possible. Now, please go."

Lupita and Keon hobble off in the direction of the plane. Raine grips her bō staff and runs to Niya, who is standing alone, her face still expressionless.

Fighting ferociously, Rashid and Qarinah seem to be evenly matched. She slashes with her shortswords as he moves his batons to counter. Rashid spins a baton to distract Qarinah as he thrusts the other. She sidesteps and advances, thrusting her sword toward his face. With the sword mere inches from his cheek, Rashid raises his baton to block the move. He twists to gain position behind Qarinah and locks his arms under hers.

"Give it up, Qarinah," he growls as he lifts her off the ground. She leans her head forward, then suddenly rears it back, smashing her head into Rashid's nose. Pain sears from his nose through his face, and he drops her.

"Come on!" he yells as blood trickles down his lip. "The nose? Cheap shot, even for you."

"You talk too much, you always have," Qarinah rasps out.

"Yeah, well." Rashid wipes at his sore nose. "You smell and you always have."

Qarinah releases a hate-filled scream and lunges at Rashid, then the two of them burst back into the fray.

Xolani and Xaden continue to battle not far from Rashid and Qarinah. He pulls chunks of rock from the mountain side, heaving them at Xaden. Xaden spins, twists, and flips with ease as he dodges the stone projectiles. Arms getting heavier, Xolani continues to push through the fatigue and pulls up a huge chunk of earth into the air. He lifts his arms, raising the huge floating boulder and sends it hurtling at Xaden.

"After all these years," Xaden says as he prepares to move, "you still fight in the same predictable way."

"Predict this!" Xolani swiftly crosses his arms and opens them again. The massive boulder explodes into a thunderous assault of jagged little pieces.

Xaden lowers his head in an attempt to hold his ground. But the force of the pelting rocks pushes him back. Xaden raises his head as the momentum of the rocks slow, throwing his hand up as blasts of fire swirl into his face. He vanishes, reappearing behind Xolani and wrapping an arm around Xolani's neck. With a vicious snarl, he plunges a dagger into Xolani's side.

"See, Xalen? Predictable. You never learned to watch your back." Xaden twists the knife before yanking it free and releasing Xolani. Xaden watches his brother stumble forward before following closely and landing his fist on the fresh wound. Xolani groans and grabs his side. After slicing through the back of Xolani's leg, Xaden sheaths the knife. Xolani takes an uneven step as he falls to his knees, his hand still pressed to his side.

Xaden strolls around him like a vulture circling his next meal. "You think you're something special? Well, you're not."

"Is that what all of this is about?" Xolani says with a grimace. "Revenge, because you're jealous?"

"You think this is about you? You're nothing!" Xaden's skin flushes, his nostrils flaring with every breath he takes. "I was stuck in a void of nothingness, with nothing and no one, for years. So, this? This is so much bigger than you. But since we are here, we can finish what was started long ago, brother." He laughs manically, grabbing Xolani by the vest as he pulls his dagger out of its sheath.

"Xaden!" Qarinah calls from a distance.

"What?" Xaden shouts, stopping abruptly to turn his head to see Qarinah was walking towards him. Rashid laying in a limp heap on the forest floor behind her.

"We need him alive."

"I don't care!" Xaden shouts, turning to glare down at Xolani with wild wide eyes.

"Xaden, we need his body and we need to go. The sun is rising and the dampening cuffs will release soon," Qarinah pleads.

Xaden continues to stare intensely at Xolani, then he moves his arm in a circular motion, causing a fractured purple circle to form beside them. Xolani looks through the circle and sees the Lumastar on the ground. Xaden pulls Xolani to his feet and tosses him through the portal. Before he and Qarinah follow through. Xaden picks up the Lumastar and then locates Niya, who is standing still despite Raine's best efforts to free her.

"Come to me!" Xaden yells.

Niya begins to walk toward him, and Raine fails to hold her back. Raine pleads and begs, but Niya continues toward Xaden. Raine puts all her weight on Niya but smacks right into the dirt as Niya vanishes and then appears next to Xaden. Xaden kneels down and moves in close to Xolani's face.

"I have you, the Lumastar, and your half-fugenie child," Xaden says smugly. Xolani swings his fist but only connects with air as Xaden moves out of the way.

"Pathetic," Xaden spits. He looks toward Qarinah before heading to the portal. He lifts Xolani to his feet and pulls him forward as they move toward the portal. Raine sprints and jams her bō staff into the dirt, catapulting forward. She lands a kick in the middle of Xaden's back, propelling him through the portal. Niya follows him as Qarinah gives Raine two quick blows to the chest, sending her flying back.

"Ta-ta for now," Qarinah says with a twisted smile as she looks at Xolani and places her hand on the ground.

"Niya!" Xolani yells as he moves to get up. The ground loosens and starts to liquify underneath him and Raine. Their bodies shift into the sinking sand. They struggle to keep their balance and slowly start to sink into the earth. They tug and lift their feet, but with every movement, they sink deeper into the shifting dirt.

Raine and Xolani yell for Niya, but she stands emotionlessly in the threshold of the portal as her parents sink further into the sand. They struggle with all their might, but every second sees them descending deeper into the sinking ground.

"Xolani!" Raine yells. "We have to save her. We have to save Niya!" Raine's head is all that's visible as she continues sinking. Her breath grows raspier the more she sinks.

Xolani struggles to free himself, his pulse beating a rapid tattoo against his skin. He's unable to blink as he watches Raine sink further into the earth.

"Raine! Hold on!" Frantically, he shoots fire and water, trying to move the muddy earth from around them. But the dirt and mud pull Xolani down even faster. Fire, water, and chunks of earth fly through the air as he tries to escape the liquified grave. As he fades into the dark, descending into the muddy, earth-filled abyss, he sees Xaden's portal close. He seals his lips tight to hold his breath, but the pressure around his lungs increases as the earth tightens around him, and what little breath he has left escapes him in a gush.

Just when he's on the brink of losing consciousness, a hand grabs him by the shoulders.

"Lani, come on, buddy. I got you," Rashid says as he pulls Xolani from the soft earth.

Once he's out of the quicksand, Xolani lays on the ground and tries to catch his breath.

"Raine!" he shouts on a gasp of breath. "Where's Raine?"

"No worries, man, just breathe," Rashid replies. "I've got her, she's over here."

"I'm okay, Lani," Raine says between heavy breaths. She glances at Rashid and notices his armor is slashed and torn in several places. "What took you so long?"

"What took me so long?" he asks rhetorically. "Sorry, I stopped for coffee. Are you serious? I was struck with lightning, carried off, dropped, fought the smelly she-hag warrior princess and saved you two—twice. What have you two been doing?"

Xolani's eyes dance with happiness as he takes a moment to enjoy that his friend and wife are alive. But the image of Niya standing emotionlessly at the threshold of the portal hits him hard. He flops back, his back hitting the ground with a thud. He lays with his palm up and a hand covering his side, curling his injured leg inward as he stares into the sea of red, pink, and orange hues in the sky.

"We need to get back to the Adventurer," Xolani mutters.

Malkum coughs and they all turn in his direction. Malkum sways back and forth on his side. With Rashid's help, Xolani staggers up, and they hurry over to him. Raine gently grabs his arm to raise him to his feet.

"Malkum, we're glad you're alive."

"You humans shot me."

"That wasn't us. You were looking right at me when it happened," Xolani says.

"Either way, I have a hole that's quite painful in my back. Regenerating slowly, thanks to all of you."

"Wait, what?" Rashid asks.

Malkum simply replies in a condescending voice, "Long story. You wouldn't understand."

Raine moves closer to Malkum and reaches behind his back to remove the dampening cuffs.

"As much as I'd like to be free, I really don't feel like turning back into that bird right now. Day in and day out for centuries, I've had to turn into that thing. For once, I'd like to spend a day not as it. So, unless you want to deal with the kwane, don't take off the cuffs, please."

"Wait, aren't you the kwane? Or at least in control of it?" Raine asks.

"I'm not the kwane!" Malkum stomps his foot like a petulant child. Xolani, Raine, and Rashid take a step back as Malkum calms himself down. "Look, humans . . . I am an angel. At least, I was." He swings his head and blows at a strand of long, blondish hair, trying to move it out of his face. With no luck at moving his hair out of his face, he says, "The kwane is a demon."

"Demon?" Raine asks.

"Yep. Full-fledged, nasty, doesn't wash, will-slap-its-own-momma kind of demon. I can hear it rattling around in my head now, just waiting to be free. If I were you, I would hurry. It's not particularly friendly."

Raine frowns. "If it's a demon, and you're a, I mean, used to be an angel, how are you both . . . I mean . . . why are you both?"

"Punishment," Malkum says simply. "I, being a creature of light, am banished and forced to live eternity here, during the night. And its punishment, being a creature of night, is to live during the day."

"Punishment for what?" Rashid blurts.

"Not that it's any of your business, but I tried to overthrow the Creator."

Rashid, Raine, and Xolani all exchange glances.

"Don't judge me! You don't know what it's like to live your days serving someone, only to have that someone go on and on and on about their newest creations and how wonderful and how magical they are. Bunch of bone sacks. Nothing special about any of you."

"You sound jealous," Rashid mumbles under his breath.

"What if I am?" Malkum snaps.

"Look," Xolani says sternly. "We're getting off topic. Are you able to tell us where Xaden went?"

"Look, flesh pot, why should I tell you anything else? You're not in charge of me!"

"Please, we don't have time for this. He has our daughter," Raine pleads.

"Okay, okay." Malkum sighs and rolls his eyes. "Xaden is going to Nuhana. Seems he and your father are working together."

"How do you know this?" Xolani asks.

"I told you. I'm an angel. Or rather, I used to be an angel . . . Xaden had control of the kwane, not me, which gave me access to see into his mind and I saw . . . never mind, you don't want to know what I saw. Wish I didn't see what I saw." Malkum stares off into the distance with a blank expression before jumping back into the conversation. "You will find him at your father's palace. You need to understand, I was merely a conduit to pull the Lumastar into this plane of existence. It is a living thing, with unlimited power, that they intend on using as a battery. If they anger it, the power inside the Lumastar will be unleashed, and your world will end."

"Do you know how they plan on extracting its power?" Xolani asks.

"Your father created a device that is designed to drain power from the Lumastar. You need to free it."

"Thank you, Malkum," Raine says. "Are you sure we can't take those cuffs off you?"

"It's okay. The sun is rising. If I take these cuffs off while daylight hits me, the kwane will be set free. You don't want that. I'm sure the cuffs will lose power at some point. When you live for eternity, you learn to be patient." A clicking sound can be heard as the dampening cuffs release and fall to the ground. Malkum brings his arms forward, raising his hands slowly.

"Go," he says as he looks at them with concern in his voice. "I will resist as long as I can." He grabs his stomach, writhing in pain as he begins to transform back into the kwane.

Raine and Rashid grab Xolani underneath his shoulders and hurry through the lightning forest. The frightening screech of the kwane follows them. They move swiftly, but the primal call of the beast hovers over them through the lightning trees. They continue onward as the kwane's shadow creeps over and passes them.

"There's the jet!" Raine yells as the Adventurer comes into view. The distance to the Adventurer is only yards away, but for them, it feels like miles. With each step toward the Adventurer, time seems to slow down. A slight heaviness settles in their stomachs as they worry over their current path. They all look ahead to the Adventurer, hoping none of them are snatched up as collateral damage by the kwane.

As they approach and make it onto the Adventurer, they scramble to the back and make it up the ramp. Raine sprints past Lupita and Gibbon as she jumps up into the cockpit and furiously begins flipping switches to start the take-off sequence. Gibbon and Lupita look at the three of them with sad and confused eyes as the ramp closes and the airlines of the plane pop and hiss from the released pressure on the landing gears. Rashid helps Xolani into his seat before moving into his own. Frantically, they secure themselves to their seats.

"Lani, Raine, I—" Miss Lupita starts to say before Xolani cuts her off.

"Gibbon, we need to go. Now! The kwane is circling overhead. We need to move."

Gibbon hurries to the front and plops into the pilot seat. He toggles the ignition switch, and the engines give a thunderous roar. Their weight sinks into their seats from the gravity pushing down on them as the plane starts to ascend. The morning sun rises on the horizon from the cockpit windows as they clear the tree tops and begin to fly forward. As Gibbon pushes on the throttle, a loud thud makes them all jerk in their seats. The weight of the kwane falls on the plane, causing it to buckle in the air. The kwane's deafening scream pierces their ears while it claws and scrapes at the plane. Lightning crackles and metal rips as the lights and instrument panels begin to flicker. Gibbon pushes the throttle hard, causing the plane to accelerate fast. He twists the control wheel, sending the plane into a barrel roll before straightening out and twisting it again in the opposite direction. Gibbon pulls the control wheel and launches the plane straight up into the sky. They soar higher and higher until they hear a clinching release sound. Raine presses a button on the console, releasing a barrage of flares from the rear of the plane. The kwane flaps its massive wings and maneuvers through them.

"Hang on," Gibbon says as he levels off the plane. "It's off, but I think it's on our six." As soon as Gibbon finishes his sentence, bolts of lightning alternate heavily at each side of the cockpit, missing them by mere inches. Gibbon dodges the assault as he turns, pushes, and pulls the control wheel. They swing from side to side in their seats as the plane hovers and maneuvers away from the kwane's attacks. Rashid's face turns various shades of green as he fights to keep his last meal inside.

"Gibbon, get us out of here!" Xolani says.

"I'm trying, sir. I just can't seem to shake the beast!" Gibbon thinks for a second. "There is one thing, but—"

"Do it," Xolani snaps.

"Sir, I don't think you understand, the Mach-15 core hasn't been tested yet!"

"Test it!" they all yell in unison.

Gibbon flicks a row of switches, then pushes the throttle to max. A loud roar comes from the engine before an explosive thunder clap is heard. They're launched back into their seats by the extreme gravitational force as the plane bursts into the distance, leaving the kwane in the wake of the Adventurer's long-fading jet stream.

Chapter 10: *The Plan*

The roar of the Adventurer's engines soften to a gentle purr as Gibbon eases off the throttle, and the plane coasts through the morning sky. Relieved that their lives aren't in immediate danger, they all breathe a sigh of relief. Xolani, Raine, and Rashid tells Gibbon and Lupita what they've learned from Malkum. Lupita calls out to Raine and Xolani with a heavy heart. They look back, and before she can utter a word, they ask in unison, "Where's Keon?"

"Niya," Lupita says with tears in her eyes as she tries to look at them. "She just appeared, and before Gibbon and I knew it . . . she took him." There's a long silence as the words *she took him* linger heavily in the air. The low rumble of the engine adds to the thick tapestry of silence deafening all inside.

"We'll get him back," Gibbon reassures them as his voice finds its courage to fight through the silence.

Lifting her head, Lupita wipes her eyes. "Yes," she says with a smile. "We'll get both of them back."

Gibbon places the jet on auto-pilot before turning to face the group. He looks right at Xolani. "I have a course set to take us back to Nuhana, however, I'm sure they are tracking us and know we're coming. Based on your information from Malkum, it's likely they will attack us once we're in range."

"Do you know how they will attack?" Xolani asks.

Gibbon shakes his head.

"I do," Rashid says. "Well, sort of. I mostly researched things the king was interested in—details on other countries, women, but more importantly, I reported historic battle strategies."

"Interesting." Xolani crosses his arms over his chest and rests his palm on his cheek. "How does this help us?"

"King Xerxes loves to catch enemies off guard by appearing weaker than he is. Oh, and he loves to flank them, too!"

"Flank?" Raine asks with a tilt of her head.

"He distracts with some sort of head-on assault, so his secondary forces can attack the opponent's blindside.

"So, most likely, King Xerxes will send an aerial assault to intercept us head-on, which will keep us focused on the immediate threat to our front. Then, while we are distracted, he'll have another group of fighter-jets waiting to catch us off guard from our sides, as we're still fighting off the first threat. But this is all just a guess," Rashid says as he leans back in his seat.

"I can't speak on the flanking part," Xolani says. "But when I met with him, he said he was sick, and he was doing a convincing job of showing it. But now that I think on it, there was a moment where his body seemed to grow in volume. It happened so fast, I was sure I'd just imagined it."

"No one actually knows what the king's gifts are," Rashid says. "Perhaps that's one of them?"

"Raine, Gibbon," Xolani says as he unbuckles himself. He stands, but the sudden fire shooting from his wounds knocks him back a step. He works to hide his pain as he moves. "Keep piloting toward Nuhana. Tell us when something pops up on radar. Lupita, Rashid, we have about three hours. We need a plan to get us past their defenses and into to the palace."

"Lani," Rashid says as he raises his hand sheepishly. "I'm sure Lupita and I can get us to the city, but what about the inner and outer walls? They are impenetrable."

Xolani and Raine share a glance before chuckling.

"What's so funny?" Rashid asks.

"The walls won't be an issue," Xolani says as Raine shakes her head. "I used to sneak through them to visit Raine. While everyone is busy, I'll do some recon and astro-project my consciousness down to Nuhana."

"Lani, you haven't astro-projected in years. Can your body handle your mind going that far, for that long?"

"I don't know, but I need to try."

"Astro-projection?" Gibbon asks.

Xolani sighs. "It's the ability to separate one's mind from one's body. We need a way in, and scouting out the rings to use those secret entrances is the only way in. It takes discipline, practice, and focus. Since I haven't done it in some years, Raine is concerned my mind won't return to my body and I'll—"

"He'll die," Raine blurts out.

Xolani exhales loudly. "Yes, if my mind doesn't return, which it will, my body dies. I become a mind without a body, if that make sense?"

Gibbon nods.

"That's how Xaden survived," Lupita says.

"Yes," Xolani says. "In not so many words. How did you know?"

"When Xaden had control of me, I could see into the parts of his mind that weren't guarded. After your battle years ago, Xaden projected himself before the final blow. Qarinah created a partially new body from his old body with her gifts, but that body isn't complete, and he is very unstable."

"You don't say," Rashid jokes.

"His body may be organic, but it's still artificial. Even with your father's help, it took them years to get his mind back into his artificial body, but his mind is twisted and has warped into something that's not your brother."

"He has my children. I don't care if he is or was my brother!" Xolani snaps. "We all have our tasks. Let's focus on what needs to be done!"

Xolani watches as the others proceed with their respective tasks and then hobbles to the rear of the jet, Raine following behind him. He sinks down on a bench and is surprised to see her behind him.

"You're supposed to be navigating," he says.

"Gibbon has it for now. Your wounds need to bandaged," Raine murmurs.

"I'm fine," Xolani says with a forced toughness in his voice. "The blade barely touched me."

"It won't hurt to look at the wound," Raine says, mustering all her love into her voice. She reaches onto a shelf above the benches and pulls down a medical kit.

"Take off your gear. I need to see the wound."

With a grimace, Xolani goes to lift his vest. He quickly retracts his arms and hugs his torso as the pain radiates from his wound.

"The pain . . . I can't," he says as he looks at his wife. "Will you, please?"

"Lift your arms."

Xolani grits his teeth as he slowly lifts his arms and Raine carefully raises his vest. Xolani grimaces and flinches as Raine manages to get the vest over his head. His shirt is stained with blood, and some of the blood has dripped onto the bench.

"Lift your shirt, if you can."

Xolani carefully lifts his shirt, and Raine inspects the jagged, oozing puncture on his side. The wound has a light red tinge. She fumbles through the medical kit before taking out a small glass jar of goldenrod powder and several patches of a branchy, greenish-gray oak moss. Raine looks at Xolani, who's staring off into space.

"Can you lay down on your side for me?"

Xolani lays on his side, and Raine takes the goldenrod powder and sprinkles it into the wound. She then takes the oak moss and lays a little in and on the wound. Finally, she pulls out a roll of bandages and asks Xolani to sit back up.

"Sit, lay, up, make up your mind," he jokes.

Raine smiles. "I could add to the pain if you like."

They both smile wide as she wraps his midsection with the bandage. "This should help the healing and take some of the edge off."

"Thank you, my love," Xolani says as Raine kisses his forehead.

"Unbuckle your pants. I'll help you take them off."

He gives her a stern look. "I'm not taking off my pants."

She glares back at him.

"I'm not taking off my pants."

She tilts her head and stares at him as he stares back at her. They lock eyes only for Xolani to break eye contact and then start to unbuckle his pants. Raine smirks as she helps him undress, then dresses the wound at the back of his leg. Once done, he fixes his pants. and she sets the medical kit back on the shelf. He places his hand on her cheek and they kiss.

He watches as she returns to her seat in the cockpit, then closes his eyes, adjusting his feet. Slowly, he rests his hands on his knees as he begins to breath in deeply and exhale slowly. He continues to breathe deeply and exhale slowly until he falls into a meditative state.

When his eyes open, he's standing and notices the others toiling away. He turns to see himself sitting with his eyes closed, meditating.

It's been so long. I forgot what this felt like. Okay, remember . . . to travel, I just have to focus on where I want to go. The metal outer ring . . . Whoa.

He's caught by surprise as he phases through the plane's floor and into the clouds. His spirit is pulled with the wind as he thinks of the metal outer wall of Nuhana. He flows like a leaf on a river's current, seeing the rural farmland and magnificent, open countryside as his consciousness floats over each town. Small specks of people pop in and out of his view as he passes.

The clear blue skies run on for miles as the Tree Palace comes into view over the horizon. Its enormous size is hidden at first, until Nuhana and its metal outer ring comes into view. The colossal city quickly multiplies in size as Xolani nears. He lands just short of the metal outer ring and begins to look around, walking along the outer wall, maneuvering through the crowds of people, cars, and vendors. He keeps an eye out and notices where the guards are posted, noting how the defenses have changed over the years.

Once he has surveyed the walls, he moves to an alleyway and phases through the metal wall at the end of it. The hustle and bustle of the inner city surround him. People walk briskly, hurrying through the city streets. Some stop to procure an item or two from the side vendors and shops. Xolani moves quickly through the streets, careful not to exert himself. He weaves around people and objects instead of phasing through them. Reaching the wall, he moves swiftly, counting the guards on patrol. He continues along before stopping and studying a small portion of the earthy wall. After a moment, he phases through it.

On the other side of the wall, he sees a cottage. Xolani's hands go clammy as he wonders if it is his mother's cottage. He stands after a moment, contemplating if he should take a peek. Xolani shakes off the thought, but finds himself inches from the door. He moves to enter but is immediately bulldozed to the ground. Xolani rolls to recover, only to find Xaden pinning him to the ground. They wrestle for control, pushing and pulling at each other. Xaden punches Xolani in the jaw as Xolani returns the favor with a blow to the midsection. Xaden wrenches away, falling to the side. Xolani quickly stands as Xaden follows him up. They lock eyes as Xolani closes the distance between him and Xaden.

"Why did you take my children?"

Xaden mirrors Xolani. "I wanted some bonding time with my niece and nephew. Is that a crime?"

Xolani clenches his hands into fists. "I should kill you while I have the chance."

Xaden smirks. "If you had the guts for that, you would have done it already. Besides, I believe you already tried and failed. I, however, will not." Xaden lunges to grab Xolani but is tossed to the inner wall. He regains his footing before Xolani rushes forward and kicks him in the chest. Xaden hurtles backward and phases through the wall. Xolani follows through and receives a hard hook to his face. The punch makes his teeth clack together, and pain explodes across his face from another set of punches. He staggers back only to have the blunt pain of a swift kick hit his mid-section. Xaden takes Xolani and flings him like a rag doll through the crowds of people and street carts. Xolani lands unbalanced, his energy drained. He rubs his eyes as he tries to refocus. Xaden walks to him, his hands held loosely behind his back.

"Has it been that long since you've projected your mind?" Xaden asks.

Xolani stands, unresponsive, his shoulders hunched.

Xaden smiles. "Tossing you through all those people must have drained all your energy. Lucky for me, I spent years in this form. It looks like you're about to fade away, and just when we were having fun." Xaden grabs Xolani by the collar and draws his arm back. His fist flies at full force toward Xolani's face before Xolani catches Xaden's hand and twists. Xolani punches Xaden in the throat as he releases his hand. Xaden gags as Xolani grabs his shirt and pulls him into a headbutt. The force causes them both to stumble backward.

"This has to end, Xaden. What do you want?" Xolani says as he rubs his forehead.

"Your death," Xaden says through gritted teeth.

"Sorry to tell you, but that's never going to happen."

"Never say never, Xalen."

"Xalen died when I left. My name is Xolani, and if you harm Keon or Niya, I swear, I will spend the rest of my life making you pay."

"Empty threats from an empty man," Xaden says with a smile. "You may have everyone else fooled, but I see you, brother. I see to the core of you. You are still that little boy wanting the attention of his daddy."

"I don't have time for this," Xolani says. Focusing his mind on the Adventurer, he's pulled upward. Xolani looks down as Xaden tugs on his foot.

"Let's see if you'll pop, or at least rip in half!" Xaden yells up at him as his body elongates. The force pulls Xolani further into the sky as Xaden continues to anchor him to the ground. Xolani snaps back and is shot through the sky, back into his body on the Adventurer.

His eyes burst open as he falls to his knees. The pain of being stretched is quickly surpassed by the sharp fire shooting from his side and the throbbing ache in his leg. Lupita and Rashid rush to help Xolani back into his seat, both asking if he is okay. Raine overhears the commotion and turns to meet them.

"Are you okay?" she asks in concern. "You were gone longer than expected."

"I'm fine," Xolani says as he works on catching his breath. "Really, I swear. I just need to sit."

"Well, did you find a way in?" Lupita asks

"I did. I also found Xaden," Xolani says as he leans back against the wall of the Adventurer.

"How is that possible?" Gibbon asks.

"He must have sensed me with his mental gifts and projected to me."

"What did he want?" Raine asks

"What else?" Xolani chuckles. "My death."

"That sounds about right," Rashid says under his breath. "How's our entry through the walls looking?"

"We're clear. The changes they've made in the last twenty years hasn't impeded the passages I used to get through the walls." Xolani leans forward, putting his hands on his knees. "What about making it past their air defenses?"

Rashid and Lupita look at each other.

"We have a plan . . . how do you feel about parachutes?" Lupita asks.

"I'm sorry, what?"

Chapter 11: *The Fight Within*

A wall of Nuhana's sleek fighter-jets—the Nighthawks—stand between the Adventurer and its crew's mission. The Nighthawks fly in tight formation to intercept the Adventurer, firing missiles at their approaching target. The Adventurer barrel rolls, evading the incoming projectiles as it banks left with the Nighthawks following closely behind, then flies straight, swaying slightly from side to side, keeping the Nighthawks from locking in on their target. More Nighthawks arrive, swarming in on the Adventurer as they flank. The Adventurer maneuvers as best it can, but it's vastly outnumbered. The sky is painted with missiles flying through the air, aimed at the Adventurer. The Nighthawks struggle to hit their target as the Adventurer banks, twists, and rolls with automatic precision. As the number of Nighthawks increase, however, the Adventurer is unable to shake the barrage of missiles closing in behind it.

A huge ball of fire erupts in the sky as missiles engulf the Adventurer. Shards of hot, twisted metal rain from the sky as Xolani, Raine, Rashid, Gibbon, and Lupita watch safely from the ground.

"I've never abandoned a perfectly good airplane before," Rashid says. "Rest in power, Adventurer. For a second, I really thought it was going to take all of those Nighthawks."

"The Adventurer's computer was quite advanced," Gibbon replies. "In fact, I'm sure it would have been victorious if—"

"Gibbon, we need to move," Xolani commands before starting to walk briskly. The group follows him. They walk fast but are mindful not to attract attention as they weave through the hustle and bustle of Nuhana's streets. As vendors yell the sales of the day and customers chat about local events, they carefully continue onward, moving briskly through the sea of people, cars, and vendors. Xolani leads them down a narrow alleyway with no outlet. At the end of the alley, Xolani examines the graffiti-riddled wall. He can feel the group watching him intently.

"Sir, are you sure there is a passage into the Tree Palace through here?" Gibbon asks.

Xolani ignores the question as he moves his fingers against the brushed metal wall, looking for the small indentation. He leans in close, sending three quick water droplets into the indentation as he flicks his finger. After a brief pause, he flicks his finger again to send a fourth droplet into the indentation.

"Hold your breath and follow me. Don't let go," Xolani instructs as he grabs Raine's hand and motions for the rest to do the same. A portion of the wall begins to liquify. The group takes a collective breath and steps through to the other side. Lush, green grass sways with the gentle wind, covering the fields circling the inner wall leading to the Tree Palace.

"Can you move through anything?" Gibbon asks Xolani.

Xolani looks at him out of the corner of his eye. "Only natural things, nothing too refined. We should focus on the mission for now." Xolani turns his gaze toward Rashid.

Rashid steps forward. "Right. While I work on disabling the palace dampeners, Lupita and Gibbon will create a diversion south of the inner wall to draw out most, if not all, of the soldiers in the palace. Once Lupita and Gibbon give the signal, it should be safe for the two of you to move past the inner ring and make your way inside the Tree Palace. King Xerxes will most likely have the device he created for the Lumastar in his throne room —it's the only place that can generate the power he needs to contain the energy from the Lumastar. So be careful, recon only. You will be alone with King Xerxes, the Five, Qarinah, Xaden, and your kids."

"Wait," Gibbon interrupts. "I thought the Adventurer fighting and getting blown up was the diversion. Don't they think we're dead?"

"Chances are they know we're alive and we should execute the plan as such. The king has two telepaths—Xaden and Niya. I don't think either of them can read minds this far away but they can sense our presence. The plane was a tactic to buy us time. The next step is to divide their forces as much as possible, then meet up to regroup near the throne room. Agreed?" Lupita says.

The others nod. With eyes full of hope and fear, they look at each other without saying a word. Lupita and Gibbon turn and jog toward the southern side of the inner wall, while Rashid moves to the northern side. Raine and Xolani head straight for the inner wall, making sure to stay low as they run across the grassy field. They crouch, keeping their backs against the wall to wait on Gibbon and Lupita's signal.

"Did they say what the signal will be?" Raine asks between gasps of breath.

"No, but knowing Lupita, I'm sure we'll see it."

"How are your wounds holding up?" Raine asks.

"Fine," Xolani says quickly, avoiding her eyes.

"You don't have to do that," Raine says, stroking his hand.

"Do what?" he replies as he moves his hand away from hers.

"Act like you're not hurting."

Xolani crosses his arms over his chest. "I'm fine."

"I'm not," Raine says, her voice soothing as she touches his shoulder. "Your brother kidnapped our children and left us for dead. He's working with your father, who tricked us into retrieving a living power source for himself. I understand if you're not fine."

"This isn't the time, Raine," Xolani says as he turns to face her. "We need to focus."

"I am focused," Raine snaps. "But we need to talk about what's going to happen when you face your family." Raine peers down at the ground. "Lani, what if we can't save the kids?"

Xolani cups her warm cheek in his hand and looks into her eyes. "We have to," he says, matching her tone. "I don't care about the king. He threw me away a long time ago, and if he and Xaden want to blow up the world, then that's on them. But we are saving our children."

"Lani!" Raine exclaims, her eyes widening. "You can't mean that."

"Mean what?" he says with a tilt of his head. "That we'll save the kids? Of course, I mean it."

"No, that you would just let the world blow up."

"You and the kids are my world. I'm not about to let either of those fools take you away from me. You are all my first priority, not the world."

Loud explosions cascade around the southern part of the wall.

"What is it with that woman and explosions?" Xolani mutters as the explosions continue to boom and echo. "Guess that's our cue."

Raine takes Xolani's hand and they leap up.

"I fell in love with your compassion and willingness to help every and anyone," she says. "This isn't you speaking. I know you're hurting, but we can save the kids and stop them, too."

Their eyes lock and they communicate without saying a word. Xolani places his hand on the inner wall, causing it to shift into a tunnel big enough for them to crawl through. They move through the tunnel as it closes behind them.

When they emerge, they see various trees and plush grass surrounding the gigantic Tree Palace. They hurry forward, stopping when they spot a multitude of guards running in the direction of the explosions. Once the path is clear, they continue toward the palace, using the trees for cover. From the corner of his eye, Xolani notices his mother's cottage. His feet cement to the ground, holding him in place as he contemplates going over to the cottage.

"Lani," Raine whispers loudly from a distance. "What are you doing? Come on."

Xolani shakes off the feeling and hurries to catch up.

When they reach the Tree Palace, he moves his hands over parts of the unique structure.

"The metal in the structure is too processed," he says. "I'm not able to manipulate it."

"HEY YOU, HALT!" a lone guard yells as she points a long-barrel rifle at them and inches closer to them. "HANDS UP! NOW!"

Raine and Xolani turn slowly, their hands raised in the air.

The guard keeps her rifle pointed at them as she pulls a radio from her hip. Bringing it up to her mouth, she says, "Intruders located in east quadrant near the Tree Palace. Request backup. Over."

"Essential units investigating disturbances in south quadrant. Take intruders to main lock up. Over."

"Copy that." She clips the radio back on her hip and motions with the rifle. "Okay, move!"

Raine and Xolani take a few steps forward, then suddenly, Raine turns and pushes the guard's rifle up, pulling it toward herself. The guard stumbles forward, and Raine delivers a stiff right hook to the guard's jaw, knocking her out.

"Now what?" Raine shakes her hand, wincing from the pain.

Xolani stands wide eyed and smiles. "You tell me. I'm following your lead now."

Raine smiles, hunching her shoulders. "Punching her out was as far as I got in my planning." She places the butt of the rifle on the ground and leans on it.

"I have an idea. Help me." He bends and starts undressing the guard.

Raine pushes him. "Have you lost your mind? What are you doing?"

"Taking off her uniform, so you can wear it."

"Oh." Raine's cheeks flush as she helps him undress the guard. "If I wear her uniform, I can escort you right into the throne room."

"Correct."

"Why didn't you just say that?"

Xolani rolls his eyes and continues to disrobe the guard.

Once they have the guard's uniform off, Raine quickly changes into it. Xolani aims his hand toward the unconscious guard and shifts the dirt around her to pack it tight around her body. He uses a small amount of dirt to cover her mouth, then he and Raine make their way through the Tree Palace. They move with caution as they make their way closer to the throne room. Raine notices the once-deep purple walls are now a pale lavender with flashing strikes of lightning flowing through them. She motions for Xolani to look.

"We need to hurry," he says.

They navigate down the halls until they reach the hallway that is vastly bigger than all the rest. Crouching, they slow their pace as they head to the enormous door that leads to King Xerxes' chamber. Raine and Xolani jump back and flee around the corner as the throne room doors creak open. Haygena and the rest of the Five emerge from the off-white light radiating from the throne room. Xolani and Raine watch as they take their spots along the walls. Haygena stands at attention in front of the throne room doors.

"I thought it was too easy getting up here," Xolani whispers.

"What should we do? We can't fight your sister and the rest of the Five."

"Unfortunately, I don't think we'll have much of a choice."

"What now?"

"I thought I told you two to recon only?" Rashid's voice says from behind them.

Raine and Xolani turn to see him, Lupita, and Gibbon standing behind them.

Raine grins, "Great timing."

Lupita smiles. "Well, we would have been here sooner but Gibbon insisted we stop and grab some things, here." She hands Raine a wooden bō staff and Rashid a pair of batons. "We rushed out of the jet so fast, we didn't think to grab any weapons." Gibbon hands Xolani a sheath with a pair of katanas in it.

"Great thinking," Xolani says as he takes the sheath from Gibbon.

"Almost," Gibbon answers with uncertainty in his voice. "Whenever there is a threat to the palace, two of the Five are supposed to go and investigate with the guards." He peeks around the corner. "Something's not right if they're all still standing there."

Rashid puts his hand on Gibbon's shoulder. "We knew they'd be expecting us, so let's not disappoint. I disabled the systems blocking our gifts, so we should be on par with the Five."

"Not really," Gibbon says with fear in his force. "They are five highly skilled warriors who have been training for years. We have what? An old lady, two farmers, a scholar, and me—a chauffeur."

"Don't underestimate us or yourself, my friend," Lupita says. "We've accomplished so much already. Don't let your fear stop your potential. Besides, I think I might have a way past them." She leans in and whispers something in Gibbon's ear.

Rashid looks on with a grimace, and Xolani and Raine are equally puzzled.

"This can't be good," Xolani whispers to Raine as Gibbon shakes his head and repeatedly mutters, "No."

But as Miss Lupita continues to whisper to him, he slowly seems to come around to her plan. She eases back from Gibbon.

"This, is not your fight. You three must stop Xaden. Gibbon and I will distract the Five."

Before anyone can protest, Gibbon and Miss Lupita sprint around the corner and down the hallway toward the five warriors.

Haygena spots them immediately and yells, "Get them!"

Gibbon and Miss Lupita come to a screeching halt, turn around, and bolt back down the hallway. They turn away from Raine, Xolani, and Rashid, who are pressed against the wall as four of the Five follow them out of sight.

"That woman never ceases to amaze me," Xolani says.

"Should we go help them?" Rashid asks.

Xolani laughs. "I have a feeling they aren't the ones who will need help."

The three move around the corner. Haygena stands at the end of the hallway, ready for a fight. Xolani motions to Raine and Rashid to stand back as he walks forward.

"We can talk this out, Haygena," Xolani calls down the hallway.

Haygena smirks. "Why should I want to talk it out?"

"Because King Xerxes and Xaden have my children and are going to destroy the world."

"That's noble for a coward and a liar! You killed Xaden years ago and ran away!"

"That's not true. Please listen to me, Ada."

Fury flashes in her eyes. "My name is Haygena."

"Your name is Ada. Remember who you are. Xerxes is a liar and is using you."

"The last time we met, I told you no one disrespects King Xerxes. No one!" She reaches behind her and pulls an axe with a black chain and hook for its handle over her shoulder. She points it at Xolani, daring him to approach her. He begins to walk, but the soft touch of Raine's hand on his shoulder stops him.

"I know you've got this, but you don't have to," she murmurs, gently pulling him back. "I'm here."

Xolani shakes his head. "What are you doing?"

"Cognitive recalibration," Raine says with a smile as she lunges toward Haygena. She positions her bō staff and strikes.

Haygena grabs the bō staff and uses Raine's forward force to propel Raine against the chamber doors. Raine twists to land her feet on the door, then launches herself back at Haygena. She spears Haygena to the ground and rolls to her feet just as Haygena jumps up, swinging her axe at Raine. Raine lifts her bō staff to counter as the axe's chain wraps around the staff. Haygena pulls the chain, making the staff fly from Raine's hands and clatter to the floor. Haygena swings the axe in a figure-eight motion as she closes the distance between her and Raine. Launching herself at Haygena, Raine uses her momentum to drop down and slide across the floor, letting her hands trail behind her as she absorbs the metal properties in the floor. She pushes herself up, sparks flying off her now-metallic skin as she blocks the swinging attack from Haygena's axe. Haygena whips the axe at Raine, who allows it to wrap around her arm. She jerks her arm, but Haygena resists and pulls against Raine's force. Raine steps closer, wrapping more of the chain tighter around her arm until she and Haygena are face to face. They grunt and pant, then Raine rears her head back and headbutts Haygena. Haygena crumples to the floor, knocked out by the blow. Raine release the axe and lets it drop to the floor as she returns to her normal state. Xolani and Rashid hurry over.

"Are you okay?" Xolani asks.

Raine wipes the sweat off her brow. "Yeah, I'm good."

"Haygena won't be," Rashid says with a grin. "She's going to have one hell of a headache when she wakes."

Xolani looks over to the door. "Hey, are you able to open the door?"

Rashid looks at it for a second. "The doors only open for those with gifts, but you should be able to open it. I think it will open if you blast it with a quick burst of air."

Xolani rolls his eyes and shakes his head before stepping back. He turns to the side, inhaling and exhaling slowly as he crouches. Raising his arms in front of him, he expels three short bursts of air at the door. The first blast leaves a circular indentation dead center, the second deepens and widens it, and the third cracks the doors wide open.

"I didn't say to obliterate the doors," Rashid mutters.

"You said to blast them."

"Not literally, a tap or two would have done it."

"Whatever, the doors are open. Let's go."

Chapter 12: *A Family Affair*

Xolani creeps forward, keeping his hands up, palms facing forward as his eyes dart around the room. He catches a glimpse of Rashid following closely beside him. Rashid's brow is wrinkled and he's breathing heavily. Xolani shifts his focus to Raine, who walks with narrowed eyes, evaluating the room for threats as they walk down the long, purple carpet, but the huge room seems to be empty. Instead of King Xerxes' throne, a huge machine with lightning firing out the top of it to the ceiling stands on the dais. The smaller thrones are also gone, and large cables and wires cover the floor. The walls are very pale, lavender-white and violent flashes of lightning course through it. The faint rumblings of thunder are now-violently loud thunderclaps. They head to the machine to examine it.

"This doesn't feel right, Lani," Raine says. "Where are the kids?"

"I wish I knew. Rashid?"

"Your guess is as good as mine." Rashid shrugs. "They all should be here, but since they're not, we might as well disable and destroy this thing."

Xolani and Rashid begin looking over the various cords, diodes, receivers and electrodes. Raine stands a few feet away from them, shuffling slightly as she looks at the machine.

"I don't even know why I'm looking at this thing," Raine mutters. "I'm going to watch the door in case someone comes in."

She moves away from the machine and watches the demolished door.

"I see some things haven't changed," Rashid whispers to Xolani as a section of the wall behind them slowly rises.

"She's just worried about the kids."

"I'm sure." Rashid says, "Hey, is it just me or does this machine looks like a huge generator?"

"You're right, but why build a generator?" Xolani replies. "The Lumastar is energy, why not build a containment battery or something?"

"Maybe," Rashid says after he takes a moment to think. "They could be trying to amplify the Lumastar. You know, to . . . create . . . more . . . pow—" Rashid slumps over onto the machine. A small dart sticks out of his neck. Xolani calls out to Raine, but the warning is a second too late as he sees his wife fall to the floor. A stinging pain pierces into his own neck, and he lifts his hand, feeling the dart. He shifts his weight to move, but his legs buckle and he collapses to the floor. Xolani manages to turn onto his back before losing all feeling in his body. The last thing he sees before slipping into unconsciousness is the lightning shooting across the ceiling.

* * *

Xolani slowly awakens to find himself on an angled table. Turning his head slowly, he looks around to see Rashid and Raine restrained to similar tables, each positioned to make a circle around the machine. King Xerxes stands at the console on the machine in front of him. Xolani tries to move his legs, but there are restraints on his ankles and shins. He then notices the weight of heavy metal straps over his forearms to his wrist. He wrests his arms but to no avail.

"You can stop struggling," King Xerxes says. "You won't break the restraints. They dampen your gifts."

Xolani looks up at his father. "Where are my children?"

"Calm down and get the bass out of your voice. Your half-breeds are fine. Keon is restrained on the opposite side of you. I had thought of using the dampening bands on him but why waste them on a gift-less fugenie, even if he is only half?"

Xolani clenches his fist as anger swells inside him.

"As for Niya, she'll be along shortly with Xaden and Qarinah. I had them fetch the Lumastar from the containment unit outside.",

Xolani's nostrils flare. "You left her with that sadistic—"

"He's your brother and her uncle. Family is important, Xalen." Raine, Rashid, and Keon begin to awaken as King Xerxes continues talking. "You do remember what family is, right?"

"Funny, I thought Ada was family. But look what you did to her. And let's not forget that Mom is family. I saw her shack, how's she?"

King Xerxes turns and faces Xolani, his body tripling in size. His legs and arms elongate as his body mass grows. He grabs Xolani, pulling him and the table into the air.

"You speak of things you know nothing about," King Xerxes says. "Your mother is not who you think she is, so I suggest you stay in your place, boy, or I will put you there myself."

"For a sick man, you seem to be doing well. Is the Mother Tree really dying or was that another lie?" Xolani says with sarcasm.

"No, I'm not dying. To prove it, maybe I should squish you like a bug."

"I thought Xaden was doing all your dirty work?"

"He's just a pawn, like you," King Xerxes says as he tightens his hold on Xolani. "I needed the Lumastar to be retrieved for a new sustainable way to power the city. The Lumastar is perfect."

"Why involve me and my family?"

"I needed someone who was expendable and able to get the job done." King Xerxes rips the metal restraints off the table. "If you didn't succeed, Xaden was my back up."

"You are a monster. Is there anything you care for?"

"You will never understand the responsibility," King Xerxes says with a sneer. "The pressure . . . everything I've done is for the legacy of this family and the people of Nuhana. Be glad you will never know the pressures of the crown. The people think I have forgotten them, but I will bring sustainable energy to Nuhana."

"The Lumastar is alive!"

"You think I didn't know that, boy? This is for the greater good. My machine will learn to generate power like the Lumastar as it extracts the eternal life essence from it."

"You know it's a living being and you still choose to harm it."

102

"Enough! I will take care of it and Xaden, but first you." King Xerxes uses both hands to hold Xolani. "Funny thing is, I expected Xaden to let the kwane finish you off even though he needs your body, but no matter. I guess if you want something done right, you have to do it yourself."

Xolani tries to hold in the pain as King Xerxes tightens his grip on the table. But the pain becomes too much, and he yells in agony. Raine cries out his name, and Rashid can barely watch his friend screaming in anguish.

Tears roll down Keon's face as the sight of his father fading away at the pressure of King Xerxes' grip overwhelms him. His heart pounds in his young chest as his adrenaline rises. His restraints grow tighter around his ankles and wrist until the sound of the metal restraints snapping echoes through the throne room.

"Let go of my dad!" Keon yells in a booming voice.

They all turn their heads to look at Keon as he grows in size and towers over them. Keon swings his arm and swats King Xerxes into the air. The king flies straight across the room, his enormous form deflating until he crashes to the floor and releases Xolani. King Xerxes wipes his cheek as he stands up. He quickly closes the distance between him and Keon as he grows to match Keon's size, each step he takes shaking the room.

"Cheap shot, boy. Let's see what you can do face to face."

They lock arms and grapple, their feet shuffling and skidding as they both try to gain ground against the other. Xolani scurries past, weaving through their feet toward Raine. He hurries to free her as the room shudders and shakes around them. Shards of the metal floor fly through the air as the battle between the young and old goliaths continue. He frees Raine and then shoots over to Rashid.

"Can you shut down the machine?" Xolani asks Rashid once they get him out of the restraints.

"I guess we'll have to see, won't we?" Rashid replies as he rubs the bruises on his wrists. He moves to the panel and begins working.

Raine looks to Xolani. "Okay. Keon got his gifts and is fighting your father, now what?" There's such a wryness in her tone that Xolani can't help but smile.

Before Xolani can answer, multiple gunshots boom through the throne room. Instinctively, Raine and Xolani move to save Keon. To their surprise, Keon begins to shrink back down to normal size. King Xerxes clutches his chest as he shrinks back to his regular size. Xolani, Raine, and Rashid turn their heads to the source of the shot and see Xaden standing in the open panel, his gun at his side. Niya and Qarinah stand next to him with the Lumastar levitating just above them.

"Why?" the king croaks as he stumbles forward and falls to his knees.

"Checkmate, Father," Xaden responds with an evil smile. "This little pawn is ready to become royalty!"

Shock crosses the king's face as Xaden lifts the gun and aims it at him. He fires a single shot that seems to ring for an eternity as it whizzes through the air and hits its target. King Xerxes' arms fling forward as his body flies back onto the floor from the force of the bullet.

"Qarinah," Xaden says. "Make sure he's dead. Niya, put the Lumastar into the machine. I need the rest of you to stand together near the doors —what's left of it. Except you, Xalen. I have something special planned for you."

When no one moves, Xaden's voice turns threatening. "I will have Niya torture herself if you don't move. Now!"

Xolani watches Raine, Keon, and Rashid move slowly toward the doors.

Xaden grins widely. "Great, now sit down and shut up." Once they near the doors, Raine grabs Keon and hugs him tight before they all sit down. Xaden waves his gun at Xolani, signaling at him to follow.

"Yep," Qarinah yells from across the room. "He's dead!"

Xaden smiles as he leads Xolani to the table Raine was strapped to. He tilts his head toward the table and motions with his eyes for Xolani to get on it. Xolani carefully swings his hurt leg onto the table as he pulls the rest of himself up. He lays back, masking his tortured side and battered leg the best he can as Xaden secures the restraints around his limbs. Xaden attaches a medical lead to Xolani's temple, shoulder, and chest.

"I'll be right back," Xaden says with a sinister smile. "I just need to check on our other patient." He goes to stand by Niya and Qarinah next to the panel.

Raine leans back against Rashid. "What's the plan?"

"Plan?" Rashid says with a wrinkled brow.

"Yeah, any ideas?"

"No."

"What do you mean, no?" Raine asks, tilting her head slightly.

"I mean, no, as in I don't have a plan. Why do you all keep asking me for plans and strategies?"

"Because you're the strategist!" Raine snaps. She quickly covers her mouth and looks to see if they've caught the attention of their captors. Xaden continues to work on the panel with Qarinah. "Isn't that what you do?" Raine whispers.

"It's not all I do," Rashid mumbles under his breath.

Raine pinches the bridge of her nose. "Are you serious right now, or are you twelve? We need to figure something out to stop them and get us all out of here."

"I don't think you should be asking me. It looks like Keon has it covered."

She turns to see a shrunken Keon running stealthily toward Xolani. She whisper-yells his name but he's too far to hear her. When he reaches Xolani, he grows back to his regular size and begins to unfasten the restraints.

"Thanks, son," Xolani says. With his hands free, he puts his hand on Keon's shoulder. "Wow, you got really big and really held your own out there. You're awesome."

Keon smiles and finishes undoing Xolani's leg restraints. Xolani is instantly reminded of the wound on his side as the pain burns from him struggling to roll off the table. The back of his leg calls out in misery as he falls onto it with all his weight. Wincing, he works through the discomfort.

"Are you okay, Daddy?"

Xolani nods and puts his arm around Keon's shoulder, motioning for them to sneak toward the doors. Keon tries to move swiftly but finds it a struggle to hold Xolani's weight. They do their best to keep a low profile as Xolani staggers.

Xolani catches a glimpse of Raine as he and Keon quietly hobble over to her. They lock eyes for a moment and all his pain drifts from his mind. Her comforting smile keeps his focus before a sharp fire sensation pierces Xolani's shoulder blade as he swivels and falls to the floor. With the familiar sound of Xaden's gun left ringing through the large room.

Chapter 13: *Awaking*

White-hot pain shoots through Xolani's body as the bullet breaches the flesh of his shoulder. The force of the bullet sends him falling to his back, the hard floor welcoming him with an even harder thud.

Raine screams as Keon kneels helplessly beside his dad, then rushes forward with Rashid on her heels, but before they can reach Xolani, Xaden points his gun and motions for them to back up and sit back down.

Xaden moves toward Xolani. "You refuse to make this easy." He aims his gun at Xolani, his finger on the trigger.

Qarinah places a hand on Xaden's arm. "We still need him alive. His body won't be any good if it starts decomposing."

Xaden reluctantly pushes the gun's hammer back in place and returns the gun to its holster. He glares at Xolani, holding his newest addition to the growing collection of wounds. Running his tongue over his teeth, he makes a smacking sound as he crouches to eye level with Xolani. "I commend your efforts, but I need a body. I was really hoping for yours, however I just need one with our genetics. I'd rather not go through puberty again, but I can use your half-breed son here," He quickly glances and sends a wink to Keon. "I could also easily use Ada or Niya. Don't think I don't have options. I will make you watch as I become one of them and you lose what you love."

A fractured purple portal forms underneath Xolani and Keon, sucking them through and dropping them next to Raine and Rashid.

"I'm on my last ounce of patience, Xalen, so please, give me a reason. Please," Xaden says as he gives Xolani a long, hard stare. He moves back to the machine and begins to instruct Qarinah and Niya.

Rashid notices Xaden's frantic movements and frustrated body language. "I don't think they know how to use the machine."

"Are you sure?" Xolani manages to ask through the overwhelming pain.

"Not completely, but look at them, they haven't put the Lumastar in it yet, and Xaden looks like he's about to blow his top."

"You're right," Raine says with a smile. "Look at Qarinah, she keeps pointing at the king's body. Xaden must have shot him before he told them how to use it."

"This could be our chance," Xolani says. "Raine, I need you to sneak Keon out of here."

"You heard Xaden," Raine protests. "He'll kill you and use the kids instead. I'm not leaving you or Niya."

"Raine." Xolani reaches for her hand. "I will save Niya, I promise, but I need you and Keon safe."

Raine pulls back and hisses his name.

"Raine! Please, get him and yourself out of here." Xolani suddenly feels a tap on his side and turns to see Keon looking up at him with his big green eyes.

"Dad," Keon says. "I know I'm small but I have my gifts now, I can help you save Niya."

"I see you, my son," Xolani says with a warm smile. "You are a prince like no other, and a prince's job is to take over for the king when the king cannot perform his duties. Right now, my duty is to finish what was started so many years ago. So, while I am doing this, I need you to protect your mother as much as I need her to protect you, okay?"

They smile at each other.

"Lani, you're still hurt, you need me."

"I will always need you," Xolani says as he strokes her face. "But I need you both safe more."

She exhales audibly. "I don't like leaving you here."

"I know." He smirks. "But sometimes we have to do things we don't want to do. Please, go while they're still distracted." He leans closer and presses his lips to hers. For just a moment, the room seems to fade away.

"Really?" Rashid says with a hint of sarcasm. "I can take the kid if you two want to get a room or some privacy." Raine leans back up and sees

Xaden and Qarinah still working on how to operate the machine. Raine takes Keon by the hand and swiftly moves to make their way out of the throne room.

"What's the plan?" Rashid asks as he scoots forward. "It's not like he won't notice they're gone, you know."

"I assumed you'd have a plan," Xolani says with a surprised look on his face.

"I do, I just wanted to see your face."

"You're wasting time."

"I noticed Xaden has had ample opportunities to kill you."

"Good, I guess."

"What I mean to say is, I don't think he's really trying to kill you, at least not yet. I think his artificial body is falling apart and he needs yours."

"You figured that out all by yourself before or after he said it earlier?"

"Do you want my plan or not?" Rashid asks.

Xolani tilts his head slightly, and Rashid continues. "Look, anyone under his influence can be brought back to normal with some type of physical or mental trauma outside of his command, right?"

"So, you think if we get Xaden to cause me harm . . . more harm than he already has, it might be traumatic enough to free Niya from his control?"

"Yes, maybe. She hasn't snapped out of it before because she hasn't been in direct line of sight to see him defeating you," Rashid jokes.

"Thanks, man."

"Well, am I lying? Look, I can distract the evil she-hag while you take on Xaden."

"I'm starting to wonder if you like her," Xolani says with a smile.

"That's not funny," Rashid says with a frown. "Seriously, not funny. Keep talking, and I'll tell Raine who you got Niya's name from."

"Don't threaten me. Raine suggested Niya's name."

"Maybe, but I bet she doesn't know about a tall, athletic, very close female friend of yours by the name of Laniya."

"We were just friends," Xolani mutters.

"Not for lack of trying," Rashid says under his breath.

"Your killing me right now," Xolani says as he pinches the bridge of his nose. "We need to focus. Distract Qarinah and I'll take on Xaden."

"No problem, but . . ." Rashid hesitates. "Are you okay to do this? You're still pretty banged up."

"I don't have a choice. He has Niya," Xolani says as he clutches his shoulder. He grimaces as he stands slowly.

"What's wrong? Is it busted?" he yells.

"Is this a game to you?" Xaden says. He scratches his head before pulling out his gun and pointing at Xolani and Rashid.

"I told you all . . . Wait, where's the fugenie and the boy? Qarinah, go and find the boy. Now!"

Qarinah darts off and moves swiftly around Xaden and Xolani. Rashid quickly moves to block her path. He stares at her as he stands ready to fight.

"It's me again." Rashid smirks. "This time you won't get rid of me with a cheap shot to the back of the head."

"It was only cheap because you didn't see it coming." She lunges at Rashid. He redirects the momentum of her forward attacks as she drives him back to the throne room doors. He allows her to drive him into the hallway and out of the throne room.

Xaden calls out, "Qarinah!" then turns his head to call out to Niya. Without another thought, Xolani sends two blast of fire at Xaden. Xaden teleports before they reach him and reappears beside Xolani, punching him repeatedly in his stab wound. Fighting against the stiffness and immense pain, Xolani grabs Xaden's forearm and pulls him closer, tossing him over his hip. Xolani stumbles forward as Xaden opens a portal and disappears into it. Multiple tiny portals begin to open and close all around Xolani as Xaden sends his fist through the tiny holes. A barrage of fists hit Xolani almost simultaneously all over his body. He moves as best he can, reaching to cover his body as hit after hit lands in all the exposed areas. He works to counter but is unsuccessful. Xolani struggles to protect himself as Xaden continues to land punch after punch. He puts his arms up to stand ready for the next attack but loses his balance as Xaden kicks his injured leg. Xolani's legs buckle as he tries with all his might to endure hit after hit. Niya watches him blankly, still under Xaden's control. Eyes on his daughter, he shakes off the sense of defeat that had settled over him. He was not yet broken. He would get Niya to snap out of her trance, no matter what it takes. Unable to completely use his shot arm, he sends bursts of fire with his other arm through every portal that opens. After a few quick blasts, Xaden rushes out of a portal, his jacket singed. He takes it off and throws it to the ground, then rushes toward Xolani at full speed then teleports.

Anticipating the attack, Xolani twists in agony and moves to aim a right cross into Xaden's nose. Xaden dodges the punch and counters with an uppercut to Xolani's jaw. Xolani's teeth slam together as he staggers back from the force. Xaden steps forward and Xolani struggles to land a kick to the center of Xaden's chest. With Xolani's reflexes slower than normal, Xaden easily catches Xolani's foot and twists, causing Xolani to spin back toward the floor. As he spins, he sends a burst of fire at Xaden, but Xaden quickly opens a portal to send the flames through. As the portal closes, the metal around Xaden begins to lift and incapsulate him. Xolani can barely keep his eyes open from the sting of his sweat falling into them, he begins to slowly tighten the enclosed space.

"Enough, Xaden!"

"Never!"

"Enough," Xolani says as he manipulates the metal to shrink. Xaden teleports out of the capsule and appears near the throne room door. He pulls his gun from its holster and aims it at Xolani.

"You're right, dear brother," Xaden says with a sinister smile. "Enough."

Xolani turns and is frozen in place. Xaden goes to shoot but struggles to move as a force immobilizes him into place. Haygena's axe whistles as it swirls through the doorway and lodges into Xaden's back. The color drains from his face as he falls to the floor. Rashid rushes through the door as he drags an unconscious Qarinah behind him. He lets her drop to the floor.

"What did I miss?" Rashid asks.

"Nothing . . . great shot. Right on time as usual," Xolani says as he staggers forward a step.

"I aim to please."

Suddenly, they hear sparks hitting metal. Xolani turns to see the Lumastar bouncing on the floor and Niya swaying on her feet.

"Daddy," Niya says softly.

Xolani hobbles toward her and wraps his arms around her.

"I saw everything, Daddy," she says through her tears. "I felt everything. I could see everything . . . I'm sorry, Daddy. I'm sorry, I tried to resist, I tried—"

"Shh, shh, nothing was your fault, okay? Nothing," Xolani says as he consoles her. He runs his hand through her hair, stroking her head gently. "It was all him, it was not your fault." He wipes the tears from her eyes and holds her tight.

Haygena stumbles into the throne room, holding her head. "Where am I?"

Chapter 14: *Who's Next*

Hours later, Xolani, Rashid, Gibbon, and Lupita sit at a conference debriefing. Lavender walls flow down to the dark purple carpeting that line the floor. A large monitor rests on the far wall next to the door. The local news is displayed on the screen, the sound muted. Images of the explosions and the fight between four of the Five and Lupita and Gibbon flash on the screen.

Haygena walks into the room with Raine following close behind.

"How are the kids?" Xolani asks as she sits down next to him.

She takes in a deep breath. "They're both talking to counsellors. Keon is doing okay. He's a little bothered about what happened but I'm sure he'll be fine. Niya . . . Niya isn't doing as well. She was under Xaden's influence much longer. It's going to take a little while for her to get her back to normal."

"I think we'll all need some type of counseling with everything King Xerxes and Xaden did," Haygena says. "But let's move on to other matters. I spoke with the council and there will be no formal charges against Gibbon and Lupita for bombing the Tree Palace and for fighting against the crown. No charges against Rashid for killing a prince, based on the grounds that he was trying to protect the throne. The Lumastar is safe here, however, we are still looking for a way to heal the Mother Tree . . . Oh, and there will be no charges against the Raveness family as they were brought here against their will by Xaden, who everyone presumed was dead. So, all previous charges against Xalen, excuse me, Xolani, who was thought to have been executed, has been dropped. Lastly, since you, Xolani, are the oldest heir to the throne, it is yours by birthright. Outside of a blood test to prove who you are, the throne is yours, Your Majesty." She begins to bow but Xolani stops her.

"I have no claim to the throne," he says. "It should be yours. My life has led us down a different path."

Haygena smiles. "I think we can all say the same, in some form or fashion. Against my will, I have lived life as a soldier and a warrior. That's who I am now. You are the eldest. It is yours by right."

"Haygena, you know and love this land, you should be its ruler."

"I'll take it!" Rashid says loudly. They all turn to look at him. "What? You two don't want it."

Laughter erupts around the room easing some of the leftover tension.

"Actually," Gibbon says humbly, "Xolani shouldn't be next on the throne. Your mother, Lady Neyma, is the rightful heir now."

"Is Mother in that cabin on the inner wall?" Xolani asks Haygena.

"She is, but I don't think she is in the proper mindset to rule a country."

"Let's go see." Xolani exits with Haygena and Raine following close behind. Gibbon, Lupita, and Rashid remain in their seats.

Gibbon turns to Lupita and asks, "Do you think we should follow them?"

"This is a royal matter and we shouldn't get involved," she replies. Gibbon quickly turns and looks at Rashid.

"Don't look at me," Rashid says. "I agree with her, we should stay out of it."

Gibbon folds his arms and leans back in the chair.

***

Outside, on the Tree Palace grounds, Haygena, Raine, Xolani, and the kids walk toward the cabin on the inner wall. Xolani holds Raine's hand as Haygena walks beside him. The children trail behind.

"Should we be taking them to see your mother?" Raine asks.

"She's my mother, so, of course."

"I know she's your mother, but with all they've been through, and we aren't sure about everything your mother has been through . . . I'm not sure it's wise to be taking them to see her prior to us seeing her first."

"I hear you, my love, but I'm sure it will be fine." They continue to walk in silence until they near the cabin and Keon asks,

"Dad? When Miss Lupita was protecting us, she mentioned her job was to take us home. I didn't understand what she meant because we were home." They reach the cabin and Xolani knocks on the door as he answers Keon,

"I will tell you what that meant, but first, it's time to meet your grandmother."

116

Epilogue

A lone shadowy figure waits in a dark void as another dark figure appears in the distance. They float closer to meet.

"Report," the shadowy figure commands with a devilish voice.

"Mission unsuccessful," the other says in a sinister voice. "But the Lumastar is in the Tree Palace and the Scion was located."

"Excellent, where is the Scion now?"

"On the royal grounds, and now that we have the Scion . . . your plan will not be stopped."

"Yes, everything is coming together. Are the others ready?"

"They are ready and await your orders."

"I will contact them once we have complete control of the Scion. The time draws near, and the Scion's time is up."

"What should we do with the Lumastar?"

"It can stay in the Tree Palace for now. We've waited this long, we can wait a little longer. Return and I will summon you when I am ready."

"Yes, Mistress," the sinister voice says as they both fade away, leaving the void empty.

Thank you

I hope along the way of creating this book, I took the time to show appreciation to all those that helped me during the process. However, if I did not, let me start off by saying thank you to any and everyone that helped, encouraged, inspired, and assisted me in their own unique ways.

To all the readers, whether you purchased, rented, borrowed, gifted, or simply checked this book out from a library; to my loving family and friends that have supported me through every version of this book; to all those that have helped talk through ideas and concepts I've struggled with thank you.

Monique Fischer, thank you for making sure my bad grammar and poor sentence structures never held back this story.

To the coffee houses (Starbucks, Dunkin Doughnuts, Lula's Coffee Co and A Sip of Coffee Company), thank you for being safe havens for me to write and for having the best chia tea lattes.

To Barnes & Nobel and Books-A-Million, thank you for not throwing me out.

Thank you God, for giving me the ability to jot down the words I feel you've given me, the ability to stay focused and keep writing this story.

And in no particular order, thank you to Donna Walker, Corey Johnson, Mandy Grooms, Gregg Farrah, Brittany Bynum, Andre Bynum, Kellie Curry, Mark Russak, Debbie Hall and Tim Hall, for either simply listening, encouraging, pushing me, and or reading the many various versions of the manuscript.

And last but not least, thank you to Luc (My favorite son), Trinity (My favorite daughter) and Shelia (My favorite, and only wife) for being my muses and helping me bring each and every character to life.

Made in the USA
Middletown, DE
30 July 2020